God's Little Princess®

Bedtime
Devotional

_____

Given to

_____

By

_____

On this date

Published in Nashville, Tennessee, by Tommy Nelson®.

Author is represented by the literary agencies of Alive Communications, Inc., 7680 Goddard Street, Suite 200, Colorado Springs, CO 80920, www.alivecommunications.com, and The Fedd Agency, Inc., P.O. Box 341973.

Thomas Nelson titles may be purchased in bulk for educational, business, fund-raising, or sales promotional use. For information, please e-mail SpecialMarkets@ ThomasNelson.com.

Scripture quotations are from the International Children's Bible®. © 1986, 1988, 1999 by Thomas Nelson. All rights reserved.

Library of Congress Cataloging-in-Publication

Walsh, Sheila, 1956-
  God's little princess bedtime devotional / by Sheila Walsh ; written by Tama Fortner.
    pages cm
  ISBN 978-1-4003-2293-0 (hardcover)
1. Girls--Prayers and devotions--Juvenile literature. 2. Mothers and daughters--Prayers and devotions--Juvenile literature. I. Fortner, Tama, 1969- II. Title.
  BV4860.W348 2013
  242'.62--dc23

                          2013021928

13 14 15 16 17 DSC 5 4 3 2

Printed in China

www.thomasnelson.com

Mfr: R.R. Donnelley/Shenzhen, China/December 2013/PPO 9283688

God's Little Princess®

Bedtime
Devotional

Sheila Walsh

Written by Tama Fortner

Tommy
NELSON

A Division of Thomas Nelson Publishers

NASHVILLE   DALLAS   MEXICO CITY   RIO DE JANEIRO

A Note to the Parents of Her Royal Highness

Bedtime. It's the promise of rest after the hustle and bustle of the day. It's the time for winding down before it all winds up again. But it can also be so much more. Those sweet, sleepy moments before slumber slips in are the perfect time to capture your child's heart and imagination.

It's the time for sharing dreams and listening to the delights of the day. It's the time for snuggling and cuddling and little girl giggles. And it's the time for pointing a princess's heart to the One who created her.

With this book, I want to help you cherish these tender, fleeting moments of childhood. Here you'll find devotionals that point out the wonder and ways of God in words that your little princess can understand. "Good-Night Giggles and Grace" activities offer hands-on ways to make God's Word real in her life. And a soft, whispered prayer wraps everything up, just like a favorite blankie.

No matter how tired you are or how long a day it has been, I encourage you to savor these times when mommies and daddies can still vanquish every foe . . . and when hearts are wide open to the truth and love of God.

Sweet dreams!

Sheila Walsh

Contents

8

God Never Changes

Every good action and every perfect gift is
from God. These good gifts come down from
the Creator of the sun, moon, and stars. God
does not change like their shifting shadows.
—James 1:17

Day changes to night, and then it changes back to day again. The seasons change from spring and summer to fall and winter. Even royal princesses change as they grow up!

Everything in this world changes. Some things change quickly—like the colors of a sunset. Other things change very slowly—like the shapes of the mountains. But everything changes. Changes can be wonderful, or they can be sad. Sometimes they can even be a little scary.

Only one thing never changes—God! He is always strong. He is always mighty. And best of all—He always loves you. And that's something that will never change!

Good-Night Giggles and Grace

Shadows are always changing. They can be long and tall, and then short and fat. Take turns making shadow puppets on the wall with your mom or dad. Can you make a bunny? A dog? A bird? See how the shadows change as you move? Shadows may change all the time—but God never does!

Dear God,
All around me, things are changing.
But, God, You never do.
It makes me feel so safe to know
I can always count on You.
Amen.

God Made the Animals

*From the ground God formed every wild
animal and every bird in the sky. He
brought them to the man so the man could
name them. Whatever the man called each
living thing, that became its name.*
—Genesis 2:19

On the fifth day of creation, God made all the birds that fly through the air—bluebirds and cardinals, eagles and owls, and so many more. On the sixth day, God made all the animals that roam the land—lions and elephants, kitty cats and mice, and so many more.

Then God brought each animal and bird to Adam, and Adam gave them names. Just imagine seeing a giraffe or a platypus or a panda for the very first time! Do you think they all quietly waited their turn in a line?

God made all kinds of different animals, but He made people in an extra special way. You see, God made each person in His own image—including you!

Good-Night Giggles and Grace

A is for aardvark, antelope, and ant. *B* is for buffalo, beetle, and bat. Can you name an animal for each ABC? Give it a try and see!

> Dear God,
> Elephants, aardvarks, gerbils, and giraffes—
> Some of Your animals just make me laugh!
> There are so many creatures for me to see,
> But I am most thankful that You made me!
> Amen.

The Stars' Names

Look up to the skies. Who created all these stars?
He leads out all the army of heaven one by one.
He calls all the stars by name. He is very strong
and full of power. So not one of them is missing.
—Isaiah 40:26

Did you know that the stars have names? Oh yes! Scientists give them very proper names, like V838. And storytellers give them fanciful names like Orion's Belt and the Big Dipper. But God also gives them names. Each and every one of them. He even has names for the stars that no one has discovered yet!

That's how big and powerful God is. He's big enough and powerful enough to name every single star. Not one of them is missing. Now, just imagine—the God who knows and names every single star also knows you, His little princess. And best of all, He loves you too!

Good-Night Giggles and Grace

If it's warm enough, take your blanket outside, lie back on it, and look up at the stars. (If you can't go outside, look out your window, or close your eyes and use your imagination.) Pick out one special star, and give it a name of your own. If you were a star, what do you think God's name for you might be?

Dear God,
I look up at the stars, and I see
The wonderful work of Your hands.
How awesome to know and believe
You know each star, and You know me!
Amen.

God Shapes Me

But Lord, you are our father. We are like clay,
and you are the potter. Your hands made us all.
—Isaiah 64:8

Have you ever seen a potter make a bowl or a vase? He takes a big, shapeless lump of clay and places it in the middle of a potter's wheel. Then—as the wheel turns—the potter shapes the clay with his own hands into something beautiful and useful.

God says that each of us is like that shapeless lump of clay. He picks us up and places us in the middle of the potter's wheel. Then God begins to shape us with His own hands. He might round out a thoughtful heart. He might pull up a love for giving. He might even smooth off a rough edge or two. In the end, He makes something beautiful and useful—you!

Good-Night Giggles and Grace

As you think about how God shapes you, use some Play-Doh to shape a creation of your own. (Put it on a tray so you won't get your bed messy!) Make a crown or a puppy or a statue of Teddy, your favorite bear. When you've finished, take a close look: your creation is covered with your fingerprints—just as God's fingerprints are all over you!

Dear God,
Your fingerprints are everywhere,
In my smile and in my hair.
Your fingerprints I cannot see,
But I know that they're all over me!
Amen.

A Job for a Princess

"Go and make followers of all people in the world. Baptize them in the name of the Father and the Son and the Holy Spirit. Teach them to obey everything that I have told you."
—Matthew 28:19–20

Everyone has work to do. Dad does, and Mom does. Even as a princess you have work to do. Maybe your job is to make your bed, put your toys away, or take the puppy for a walk.

There are all kinds of different jobs. Some jobs are in the city; some are on the farm. Some are in big office buildings, and some are at home. But there's one job that's the same for everyone who believes in Jesus—no matter how big or small you are.

What is it? It's to tell the world all about Jesus and to teach people to obey Him. That's the job Jesus wants His people to do—even little princesses like you!

Good-Night Giggles and Grace

You probably have some chores to do here on earth, but what might your heavenly chores be? Will you help paint the sunsets or polish the halos? Will you sweep up the angel dust from the golden floors? Will you be in charge of fluffing the clouds? Have some fun imagining what your heavenly chores might be!

Dear God,
You've given me a job to do,
And I want to do it well.
I guess I should get started,
'Cause I've got the world to tell!
Amen.

✳ It's Not Fair ✳

Wait and trust the Lord. Don't be
upset when others get rich or when
someone else's plans succeed.
—Psalm 37:7

t's not fair!

Why does she get to be the princess in the play? Can't they see you're perfect for the part?

Why does he get to go first today? It's your turn to lead the line!

Why does a princess have to take out the trash? Aren't there servants for that?

Sometimes life doesn't seem fair, and sometimes it's really not! Sometimes people get things they don't deserve. Sometimes they even get things that should have been yours! "It's not fair!" you might say. Well . . . no, it's often not. But this world isn't perfect like heaven will be.

So what should a princess do when life is unfair? Take a deep breath, and don't throw a fit! Ask God to help you remember all the gifts that you *have* been given, and choose to think on those.

Good-Night Giggles and Grace

When things just aren't going your way, it helps to remember your blessings. Take a look around your room. How many blessings can you count? Can you count five or ten or even twenty? Can you count even more?

Dear God,
It's not fair; it's really not.
The thing I wanted is the thing she got!
Help me to trust You know what's best
And to realize just how much I'm blessed!
Amen.

The Wise Man's House

"Everyone who hears these things I say and obeys them is like a wise man. The wise man built his house on rock."
—Matthew 7:24

Jesus once told a story about two men—a wise man and a foolish man. The wise man built his house on rock. The storms came, and winds blew against the house. But the house didn't fall because it was built on the rock.

The foolish man built his house on the sand, which shifts and changes. When the storms came and winds blew against that house, it fell with a big *crash*!

Jesus' story is a parable. That means it's an earthly story with a heavenly meaning. The wise man was someone who believed in Jesus and obeyed Him. The foolish man was someone who heard Jesus teach but didn't believe Him or obey His words.

Be a princess who is wise—build your life on the rock of Jesus by obeying His Word, the Bible.

Good-Night Giggles and Grace

If you know the song, sing "The Wise Man Built His House upon the Rock." As you sing about the wise man, jump up and down on the floor. As you sing about the foolish man, jump up and down on the bed. Which one is sturdier? The floor, of course! So build your life on the Lord Jesus Christ!

Dear God,
I can be wise, or I can be foolish.
The choice is up to me.
So I choose to build my life on You
And be who You want me to be.
Amen.

The Greatest Command

" 'Love the Lord your God with all your
heart, soul and mind.' This is the first
and most important command."
—Matthew 22:37–38

One day one of the Jewish leaders asked Jesus which of their many laws was the most important. Jesus said that the greatest law is to "love the Lord your God with all your heart, soul and mind."

Do you know what Jesus meant? Loving God with your heart means loving Him more than anything else—just as Peter and Andrew dropped their fishing nets to follow Jesus. Loving God with your soul means sometimes giving up the things you want so that you can do what God wants—just as Abraham gave up his home to travel to the promised land. Loving God with all your mind means obeying God even when it doesn't make sense—just as Noah did when he built the ark.

God wants you to love Him with everything you've got. Why? Because that's how He loves you!

Good-Night Giggles and Grace

Make up your own sign language to help you remember this verse: "Love the Lord your God with all your heart, soul and mind." For example, for *love* give yourself a hug, and for *Lord your God* point up to heaven.

Dear God,
I will love You with all my heart.
I'll love You with all my strength and mind.
Lord, You are everything to me—
No greater love than Yours I'll find.
Amen.

The Second Greatest Command

"And the second command is like the first:
'Love your neighbor as you love yourself.'"
—Matthew 22:39

Jesus said the greatest of all God's commands is to "love the Lord your God." And the second greatest command is to "love your neighbor as yourself."

But who is your neighbor? Is it just the people who live next door to you? Yes, they are your neighbors. But when Jesus says *neighbor*, He means much more than just people who live close by. Jesus means anyone and everyone.

Loving your neighbor is like the Golden Rule—treat others the way you want to be treated. Do you want to be smiled at? Then smile first. Do you want others to play with you? Then play with the girl no one wants to play with. Do you want others to be kind to you? Then be kind to them.

When you follow Jesus' Golden Rule, you'll sparkle like gold too.

Good-Night Giggles and Grace

Think of all the different things you'll do tomorrow. Will you stay home or go to school? Are there errands to run? How many different "neighbors" will you meet? Think of a way to show the Golden Rule to each "neighbor" you see.

Dear God,
Everywhere I go each day
Help me follow Your rule
To love my neighbor as myself
At home, at play, and at school.
Amen.

Under God's Wings

*Be merciful to me, God. Be merciful to me
because I come to you for protection. I will come
to you as a bird comes for protection under its
mother's wings until the trouble has passed.*
—Psalm 57:1

Have you ever seen a mama bird gather her babies together under her wing? Mama bird knows how to keep her babies safe and warm. And the babies trust their mama to take care of them.

This is how God says that His love for you is—just as warm and safe as that cozy spot under a mama bird's wings. In good times or bad, you can always run to God, just as baby birds run to their mama, and He will keep you safe and cozy and warm.

Good-Night Giggles and Grace

You may not be a bird, but you can still hide under your mom's—or dad's—wings. Curl up under his or her arms, in the special place where it's cozy and warm. You can even make a nest from your blankets. Then say your prayers together.

Dear God,
When I am frightened I run to You
And hide up under Your wing.
I'll stay right there 'til the fear is through
And until I'm ready to sing.
Amen.

Time for Everything

There is a right time for everything.
Everything on earth has its special season.
—Ecclesiastes 3:1

God made each day with its own special times. There are times to laugh and to dance. There are times to cry and be sad. Sometimes you should be silent, and sometimes you should shout! There are times to praise God and pray, and there are times to sing. There are even times to hug.

God gave us the sun and moon to help us know the different times. When the sun is out, it's time to work and play and pray. But when the moon comes up, it's time to rest and get ready for another day.

It can be hard to stop playing and go to sleep. But remember, God made a time for sleep to begin and a time for sleep to end. Soon it will be time to play again!

Good-Night Giggles and Grace

Lie on your back on your bed, and pretend that your arms are the hands of a really big clock. As you move your hands up, down, and around, say this little rhyme:

Tick, tick, tock,
The hands go round the clock.
Time to work, time to play,
Time to sleep, after I pray.

Dear God,
There's a time to work and a time to play.
There's a time to sing and a time to pray.
I want to live my life Your way.
So thank You, Lord, for these times each day.
Amen.

Jesus Is the Light

"I am the light of the world. The person who follows me will never live in darkness."
—John 8:12

Have you ever tried to walk in the dark? It's not easy, is it? You might trip over something or stub your toe. Ouch! Walking in the dark can really hurt!

In the book of John, Jesus talks about another kind of darkness. This is a darkness caused by not having Jesus in your life. In this kind of darkness, there are lots of things to trip over too. But instead of stubbing your toe, this darkness can cause you to trip and fall into sin!

Jesus doesn't want that to happen. That's why He came into this world. He is light, and He chases away the darkness of sin. All you have to do is follow Him and obey what He teaches—then you won't have to worry about darkness.

Good-Night Giggles and Grace

Play a game of Follow the Leader with flashlights. Give Mom or Dad a flashlight; then turn out all the lights in the house. Follow your mom or dad, using only the flashlight to find your way to bed. Following the flashlight keeps you safe from stumbling. In the same way, following Jesus keeps you safe from stumbling into sin.

Dear God,
Jesus is the light of the world;
He's also a light for me.
I want to shine with His great love
For all the world to see!
Amen.

Love Your Enemies

"You have heard that it was said, 'Love your neighbor and hate your enemies.' But I tell you, love your enemies. Pray for those who hurt you."
—Matthew 5:43–44

Have you ever gotten all itchy and scratchy? It can make a princess grumpy! Now, have you ever been around a person who said or did things that made you feel all itchy and scratchy? People like that can make you grumpy too!

So what's a princess to do with itchy, scratchy people? Well . . . be nice. Yes, be nice, and ask God to help them be nice too.

Think of it this way—have you ever had someone be nice to you when *you* weren't being very nice? Maybe it was your mom or a teacher or a friend. That person's kindness probably made you want to be nicer. So try being kind to the next itchy, scratchy person you meet— she just might turn out to be pretty sweet.

Good-Night Giggles and Grace

Gently rub a nail file across your hand. Kind of scratchy and itchy, isn't it? Now rub your hand over your favorite stuffed animal. Much better! When you gossip or say mean things, you're kind of like a scratchy nail file—itchy to be around. But saying nice things and treating others politely, that makes God—and people—smile!

Dear God,
Some people are scratchy
as scratchy can be.
Sometimes those people
are . . . well . . . me!
Help me forgive them—
that's what I should do.
And please, dear Lord,
forgive me too.
Amen.

God Has Plans for You

> *"I know what I have planned for you,"*
> *says the Lord. "I have good plans for*
> *you. I don't plan to hurt you. I plan to*
> *give you hope and a good future."*
> —Jeremiah 29:11

God has plans for you. Yes, it's true!

Before you were born, He planned each and every day of your life (Psalm 139:16). And God's plans are good. His plans are to give you hope and a good future.

Of course, that doesn't mean that everything will be perfect or that you'll never have any troubles. But it does mean that God will use everything in your life—both the good and the bad—to help you on your way to heaven. That is the journey He's got planned for you—He's got it all mapped out!

Good-Night Giggles and Grace

Plan out a trip of your own. It could be all the way to the mountains or the beach, or it could be just across town or to the zoo. Use a real map to figure out how you would get there, or draw up a map that's all your own.

Dear God,
Thank You for Your plans each day—
Plans to work and plans to play.
I'll trust You to do what's best.
Now I'll close my eyes and rest.
Amen.

A Trail of Goodness

Jesus went everywhere doing good.
—Acts 10:38

D o you leave a trail everywhere you go? A trail of toys or a trail of crumbs? Some princesses are easy to find by the royal mess they leave behind!

Jesus left a different kind of trail everywhere He went. He left a trail of doing good. Everywhere He went, He healed the sick, made the blind see, and even raised people to life again! There are all sorts of ways you can be like Jesus and leave a trail of goodness and mercy behind you. Start by sharing smiles, hugs, and kind, loving words.

And there's one more thing Jesus did that you can do too! Everywhere Jesus went He told everyone all about God and how to get to heaven.

Jesus left a trail of goodness on this earth, and He hopes you will follow His example and leave your own trail of goodness too!

Good-Night Giggles and Grace

Use a roll of tissue to make a trail to your bed. As you go through each room, think of good things you can do there tomorrow. In the kitchen, check for crayons you can put away. Passing by the phone, think of someone lonely you can call. When you pass your toys, choose one to give away.

Everywhere I go, dear Lord,
I hope I leave behind
Signs of Your love—a hug, a smile—
For other ones to find.
Amen.

When Someone Picks on You

*Do not do wrong to a person to pay
him back for doing wrong to you.*
—1 Peter 3:9

Have you ever been picked on? Or has someone made you cry? Has someone ever been mean to you just because she could? It happens to everyone—even daughters of the King.

It's hard to understand why some people seem to *want* to be mean. So what's a princess to do when she's under attack? First, say a prayer and ask God for His help. Then . . . be kind.

Be kind? To *her*? Yes, be kind! That's what God asks you to do. If someone says mean words, don't say more mean words back. If someone hurts your feelings, don't hurt hers too. Talk to your parents and get help if you need it, but if someone does you wrong, don't do wrong back (1 Peter 3:8–9).

Who knows? Your kindness just might help her see how wonderful being a daughter of the King can be!

Good-Night Giggles and Grace

If someone is being mean to you, practice what you will do. Pretend it's your teddy bear who's being attacked. Ask Mom and Dad to help you to teach Teddy what to do and say so that God's kindness will rule the day! Remember what the Bible says: "Do not let evil defeat you. Defeat evil by doing good" (Romans 12:21).

Dear God,
Some people really are not nice.
It's like their hearts are made of ice.
Help me to warm them with Your love
And point them to Your Son above.
Amen.

Ask the Animals

*Ask the animals, and they will teach you. Or
ask the birds of the air, and they will tell you.*
—Job 12:7

Even in Bible times, some people had trouble believing in God. They couldn't see or touch Him, so they said He just couldn't be real. The same thing happens today. Some people find it hard to believe. But God has an answer for them—and for you: ask the animals!

Now, God doesn't mean you should stop the nearest bunny and start talking . . . that would look funny and might confuse the bunny! No, but just take a look at all the different animals and how wonderfully they are made. That bunny didn't hop itself into creation. And those birds didn't fly themselves into the sky. They were each crafted and created—made by God—from the biggest whale to the smallest bug.

So if someone asks how you know God is real, tell that person to take a long look at God's amazing animals.

Good-Night Giggles and Grace

When it's time for you to sleep, you curl up in a bed. But how do little animals go to sleep? Do owls hoot out a soft lullaby? Do lions roar instead of snore? Do squirrels rock to sleep in the sway of the trees? What do you think?

Dear God,
It's sad to know some people
Do not believe You're true.
"Ask the animals," is what You say.
Their lives are proof of You!
Amen.

Jesus Is Stronger Than the Storms

Jesus stood up and commanded the wind and the
waves to stop. He said, "Quiet! Be still!" Then
the wind stopped, and the lake became calm.
—Mark 4:39

Jesus and His disciples climbed into a boat and went out on the sea. But Jesus was tired, so He fell asleep in the back of the boat. Then came a terrible storm! The wind roared, and the waves crashed over the side of the boat! The disciples were scared. They went to Jesus and cried, "Save us!" Jesus stood up and said, "Quiet! Be still!" And the storm stopped.

When you're frightened, do just what the disciples did—go to Jesus. He is stronger than the storms—and not just the ones on the sea. Jesus can handle the stormy parts of life too—things like being afraid, having a fight with a friend, sickness, or just not knowing what to do.

Take your fears to Jesus, and He'll take care of you.

Good-Night Giggles and Grace

The disciples were tossed about by the waves, but Jesus calmed the storm. Act out this story with Teddy and your blanket. As Mom and Dad flap the blanket to make a "storm," let Teddy ride the "waves." Stop the blanket storm by saying, "Quiet! Be still!"

God, when I am frightened,
I will come to You.
You tell all little children
That this is what to do.
For all You have to say is,
"Quiet! Be still!"
And even the biggest storms
Then have to do Your will.
Amen.

Never Stop Talking to God

Never stop praying.
—1 Thessalonians 5:17

Does prayer ever seem like a hard thing to do? Maybe you just don't know what to say or how to say it. Maybe you're worried you won't get it right. Well, the good news is that prayer isn't hard, and there isn't only one right way to pray.

Prayer is simply talking to God. Some prayers are serious. You might bow your head and close your eyes. Some prayers are sad as you tell God about your hurts. You might say these prayers curled up in a chair. Some prayers are asking God to help those in need. For those you might drop to your knees and lift your hands up to heaven. Some prayers are thanking God for all He's done. You might want to sing these prayers!

And some prayers might not seem like prayers at all because you're just having a little talk with God. And do you know what? He's listening—all the time.

Good-Night Giggles and Grace

Use the "Five-Finger Prayer" to help you pray. Your thumb reminds you to pray for those closest to you, your family and friends. Your pointer finger is for preachers and teachers who point others to Jesus. Your tallest finger is for your leaders, while your ring finger—the weakest—reminds you to pray for the sick. Your pinkie is the last, so now pray for you!

Dear God,
You are my Lord and Savior.
I love You more each day.
I thank You, Lord, for loving me
And listening when I pray.
Amen.

God's Sweet Promises

Your promises are so sweet to me.
They are like honey to my mouth!
—Psalm 119:103

A promise is something that is easy to make but not always so easy to keep! Have you ever made a promise you couldn't—or just didn't—keep?

Sometimes things happen and people simply can't keep their promises. Perhaps your mom promised to take you to the zoo, but then a terrible storm came that day (although she'll probably try again soon).

Sometimes people just decide they don't *want* to keep their promises. Have you ever promised to share a favorite toy but then decided you didn't want to?

Promises are a struggle for everyone—even God's princesses! That's because people aren't perfect, and the world we live in is far from perfect too. But God *is* perfect. And He *always* keeps His promises—every single time. And that is perfectly sweet!

Good-Night Giggles and Grace

The Bible tells us that God's promises are sweeter than honey. Did you know that bees make honey from flowers? Make your own flower by coloring a coffee filter with washable markers. Spritz it with water to make the colors blend. When it's dry, you can hang it in your window and see if any bees stop by!

Dear God,
Your promises are sweet and true.
And I can always count on You.
I know You'll do whatever You say
Every night and every day.
Amen.

No Tears

*He will wipe away every tear from
their eyes. There will be no more
death, sadness, crying, or pain.*
—Revelation 21:4

Heaven is a place so wonderful, so amazing that we can only imagine how great it will be! We'll see gates made of pearls, streets of gold, and a room Jesus has made just for us. But that's not even the very best part!

In heaven, God will wipe away every last tear. There will be no more pain or sadness or crying. Darkness and nighttime will be gone. But that's *still* not the very best part!

So what *is* the very best part? In heaven you'll see Jesus, face-to-face!

Good-Night Giggles and Grace

There are some things you won't ever need in heaven. You won't need tissues because there will be no crying. You won't need bandages because there will be no more boo-boos or skinned knees. What other things can you think of that you won't need?

Dear God,
In heaven there will be no sadness,
And that's just amazing to me!
Thanks to You, I won't need a bandage,
'Cause in heaven, I won't skin my knee!
Amen.

A Princess
Always Goes Last

*Jesus . . . said, "If anyone wants to
be the most important, then he must
be last of all and servant of all."*
—Mark 9:35

Me first! It's my turn! I was here first!"

Do you ever hear words like these? Do you
ever *say* words like these? Being first *is* fun. You
get to go . . . well . . . first! Waiting your turn isn't so fun.
After all, you really want to play on the swings now!

But Jesus asks us to "be last of all and servant of all."
What does that mean? It means thinking of others *before*
you think of yourself. It means letting your friend go first
or giving her a chance to choose which game you'll play.

You see, being a princess isn't just wearing a crown.
It's being a daughter of the King and acting in a way that
will make Him proud!

Good-Night Giggles and Grace

Taking turns can be tough to do! So practice with your mom or dad as you make up a story together. First, let your mom or dad make up a line, then you make up a line. Keep taking turns until the story ends. Here's a line to get you started: "Once upon a time, there was a little princess who . . ."

Dear God,
I really like to go first—
I have to confess, it's true.
But tomorrow I'll go last
Because You've asked me to.
Amen.

God Never Forgets You

The Lord your God will go with you.
He will not leave you or forget you.
—Deuteronomy 31:6

People forget things—even princesses do!
You walk into ballet class, all ready to dance—but, uh-oh, you forgot to wear your tutu. How can you twirl in blue jeans?

And how is it again that you're supposed to tie a shoe? Does the shoelace go under or around or over? Which string do you pull through?

Mom told you to pick up your toys, but then you forgot. And taking the puppy for a walk, well, you didn't quite remember.

Yes, people forget things—big things and small things. We all do. But the Bible tells us that God never forgets, and He especially never forgets you. You are much too important to Him!

Good-Night Giggles and Grace

Play a match game to help you learn to remember. (You can use most any kind of card game for this.) Pull out pairs of cards—you could start with just three or four pairs, and then work your way up to more. Mix them up, and lay them out facedown. See if you can match the pairs. Now, where was that last one? Don't forget!

Lord, sometimes I forget things,
Like how I should tie my shoe!
But You always remember me,
And I'm thankful that You do.
Amen.

Love Is . . .

*Love is patient and kind. Love is not jealous,
it does not brag, and it is not proud. Love
is not rude, is not selfish, and does not
become angry easily. . . . Love patiently
accepts all things. It always trusts, always
hopes, and always continues strong.*
—1 Corinthians 13:4, 5, 7

"Love each other," that's what God asks you to do (John 13:34). But what does *love* mean? Is it sparkly hearts and bright red and pink flowers? Is it butterfly kisses and warm, cozy hugs? Is it snuggles with puppies and with Mom and Dad? Yes, but it's also much more.

Love is sharing your toys—one more time. It's letting someone else be the star of the show. It's not bragging when you win the crown. It's not putting others down. Love is keeping your cool, even when things are royally hard. It's loving your friends and their quirky ways. Love is trusting God and believing in His promises no matter what.

Good-Night Giggles and Grace

Are you showing God's kind of love? Try this test of your love: Wherever the word *love* appears in 1 Corinthians 13:4–7, put your name instead!

Dear God,
I'm not always patient,
And I'm not always sweet.
Sometimes I'm selfish
And stomp both my feet.
Lord, change my heart
And fill it with love—
The love that's from You,
Sent from heaven above.
Amen.

God's Little Helper

We are workers together with God.
—2 Corinthians 6:1

Princesses make great little helpers. You help out your mom, and you help out your dad. You work at school and church too. A princess has lots of helping to do! Putting away crayons and tidying up your toys. Planting flowers and pulling weeds. Playing with your baby brother and teaching him all those ABCs!

But did you know that you're God's little helper too? When you help Mom and when you help Dad, when you help your teacher and friends at school, you're also helping God—by showing them His love.

You see, God is counting on *you* to show people how much He cares. It's your hands that hug your friends and wipe away their tears. It's your feet that hurry to obey Mom and Dad. And it's your face that smiles when you say, "I'm happy to share."

Yes, you're God's little helper—helping others see how much He cares!

Good-Night Giggles and Grace

Do you know that by being Mom and Dad's little helper you're also being God's little helper? When you help others, you're helping God—by showing them His love. How can you help before you close your eyes to sleep? Put your clothes away? Pick up your toys? Ask Mom and Dad what would help them most.

Dear God,
Use my hands, and use my feet.
Show me the perfect way
To meet the needs of others
And serve You every day.
Amen.

Faith Is . . .

Faith means knowing that something
is real even if we do not see it.
—Hebrews 11:1

Some people struggle to believe that God is real simply because they can't see Him. But think about it: Do you believe wind is real? *Of course!* How about air? *Surely!* And do you believe love and joy and sadness are real? *Without a doubt.* But how can you, if you can't see them?

Well, you may not be able to *see* those things, but you can see what they do. Wind sends the kites flying, and air fills up balloons! Love is in a hug, joy in a smile, and sadness in a tear.

In the same way, you can know that God is real because you can see what He does. This world is no accidental thing. It's God who tells the sun to rise each morning and teaches the birds to sing. And it's God who makes beautiful little princesses—just like you!

Good-Night Giggles and Grace

Ask your mom or dad to fold up a paper airplane for you. Maybe they can even teach you how to make your own. Now send it flying. You can't see the air, but it's the air that keeps the plane soaring!

Dear God,
I may not see You face-to-face,
But I know that You are real.
In You, I'll always put my faith
'Cause Your love I can feel.
Amen.

No Trouble for God

David said to him, "You come to me using a
sword, a large spear and a small spear. But I come
to you in the name of the Lord of heaven's armies."
—1 Samuel 17:45

D o you know what Goliath did when David ran out to fight him? He laughed! Goliath made fun of David because he was small and young. But David knew he wasn't fighting Goliath all by himself—God was on his side! And no trouble is too big for God—not even giant trouble!

You probably won't ever have to fight a giant, but even the most royal of princesses sometimes have to do things that are hard or even a little scary. Maybe you need to tell someone you're sorry, or learn to dive into the pool, or speak in front of the whole class! Whatever you have to do, remember you're not alone. God was with David, and He'll be with you. And no trouble is ever too big for God!

Good-Night Giggles and Grace

Are there some troubles that are troubling you? Give them to God; that's what you should do! He can make your troubles pop like bubbles. When you pray tonight, tell God about your troubles. Afterward, pretend to blow "trouble" bubbles into the air, and pretend they are floating far away.

Dear God,
Some troubles are big.
Some troubles are small.
I give You my troubles, Lord.
Please take them all!
Amen.

Happy and Sad

Be happy with those who are happy.
Be sad with those who are sad.

—Romans 12:15

When you're happy, you want to share it. That's part of the fun. Just imagine if there were no one to share your joy! It wouldn't be quite so joyful, would it? And when you're sad, sometimes you just need a hug from a friend. Feeling sad all alone only makes the blues feel bluer.

That's why God asks us to be there for each other. When your friend is happy, be happy with her. And if she's happy because she got the toy you wanted, be happy for her anyway. When your friend is sad, listen and give lots of hugs. And if she's sad because *you* got the toy she wanted, be sad with her anyway.

Jesus wants you to put others before yourself. Be happy with the happy and sad with the sad—that will make Jesus glad.

Good-Night Giggles and Grace

Practice sharing happy times and sad by making faces with Mom and Dad! Take turns making happy, sad, angry, surprised faces and more. The other person should try to make his or her face match yours.

Dear God,
No one should have to be all alone,
Whether we're happy or sad.
Help me reach out to those all around
And share the good times and bad.
Amen.

Crown of Kindness

The right word spoken at the right time
is as beautiful as gold apples in a silver bowl.
—Proverbs 25:11

Do some words make you smile? Do some words make you frown? Are there some words that make you laugh? Or cry? Or even want to flip upside down?

Words are powerful things. You can use them to build people up by making them feel good. Or you can use them to tear people down by making them feel bad. You can even use your words to lead others to Jesus—or away from Him. Because you're His princess, God wants your words to be like sparkling jewels—beautiful treasures that you give to those around you.

So before you open your mouth to speak, ask yourself these questions: Will my words help or hurt? Will they make others feel stronger or weaker? Will they show Jesus' love? Will they be a sparking jewel and gift?

Good-Night Giggles and Grace

Make a paper crown. But instead of decorating it with jewels, write on it all the kind, sparkly words you can think of. Then tomorrow, see how many of those sparkly words you can give away! (And while you sleep, Teddy can wear your crown.)

Dear God,
Fill my heart with words of kindness.
Help my mouth say what is true.
Let me tell the world about Jesus
And lead others straight to You.
Amen.

A Place to Pray

*"When you pray, you should go into your room
and close the door. Then pray to your Father
who cannot be seen. Your Father can see what
is done in secret, and he will reward you."*
—Matthew 6:6

Do you know any show-offs? Maybe it's the girl in ballet who can stand all the way up on her tippy toes and wants to make sure you know it. Or your neighbor who always has the fanciest dress and just has to show it.

Well, there were show-offs in Jesus' time too. The Pharisees were supposed to help people worship God, but instead they showed off their own prayers. They would pray as loudly as they could—just to be seen!

Sometimes it's good to pray with others—at church, mealtime, or bedtime. But it's not good to pray just to be seen. God wants your talks to be between you and Him. So find a quiet spot to pray. It's the thing to do.

Good-Night Giggles and Grace

Ask Mom and Dad to help you find your own special place to pray. It could be your favorite chair or a big pile of comfy pillows. It could be up in your room or outside under the tree. It can be anywhere that works for you and God . . . but it's okay if Teddy comes too!

Dear God,
In my bed or under the stars,
It doesn't matter where we are.
Help me remember a prayer can be
A talk between just You and me.
Amen.

God Loves Us All

To God every person is the same. God accepts anyone who worships him and does what is right. It is not important what country a person comes from.
—Acts 10:34–35

Think about everything in the world God has created—so many different animals, birds, and fish. And just think of all the flowers—a zillion different kinds in a zillion different colors. And sunsets? No two are ever the same. Our God is *very* creative!

That's probably why God made people the way He did—in all different shapes, colors, and sizes. Some have blue eyes, and some have brown. Some people have black hair, some have red, and some have none at all! Each person is beautiful and precious in God's sight.

But the thing God cares most about isn't how you look on the outside; it's how your heart looks on the inside. Is it full of love? And have you chosen to follow Him?

Good-Night Giggles and Grace

Think about all the wonderful people in your life. They come in all shapes and sizes and colors—and Jesus loves them, every one! Sing "Jesus Loves the Little Children" as you thank Him for all your many different friends.

Dear God,
You made all people different.
No two are just alike.
But black or white or purple,
Each is precious in Your sight!
Amen.

Praising God

Shout with joy to the Lord, all the earth. Burst into songs and praise. Make music to the Lord with harps, with harps and the sound of singing.
—Psalm 98:4–5

Lots of verses in the Bible talk about praising God. But what is *praise*? And how is a princess to do it?

Well . . . praise is just telling God that you know how awesome and amazing He really is. It's thanking Him for every blessing that He gives you. And it's telling the world you're so glad you know Him.

A princess can praise her royal King in lots of different ways. Praise can be soft and sweet—just between you and God. Or praise can be big and bold—for the whole world to know! Whisper it softly or shout it out loud. Sing, clap your hands, or even dance—the important thing is just to praise Him at every chance!

Good-Night Giggles and Grace

Sometimes you just have to praise God with a song. So strike up your band—your "air band," that is—and make up your own praise song for God. Will you play guitar or piano? Or perhaps a heavenly harp? Be sure to get Mom and Dad to play along!

Dear God,
You are really so amazing—
I just want to shout and sing.
Thank You for all Your creation.
I praise You for everything!
Amen.

Shhh! It's a Secret Good Deed!

"Be careful! When you do good things,
don't do them in front of people to be seen
by them. If you do that, then you will have
no reward from your Father in heaven."
—Matthew 6:1

When Jesus lived on earth, some people would do good things—such as giving to the poor or helping the sick—just to be seen by others. They cared more about what people thought of them than they cared about God—or even the people they were helping. Some would even blow trumpets to make sure people saw them doing something good!

But Jesus said these people won't get any heavenly reward from God because they already have their reward from men here on earth. Jesus wants His children to give in secret so that only He knows. That's the kind of giving He rewards with jewels in your heavenly crown!

Good-Night Giggles and Grace

Secretly bless someone you love. Slip a picture in Dad's briefcase. Put a paper heart on Mom's pillow. Or give your allowance to someone in need. Who can you surprise with a good deed? Just remember: *Tip, tip-toe! No one should know!*

Dear God,
Help me keep this secret—
Between just me and You.
And quietly help others
Because You ask me to.
Amen.

✳ God's Job For You ✳

God made us new people so that we would
do good works. God had planned in advance
those good works for us. He had planned
for us to live our lives doing them.
—Ephesians 2:10

God didn't make you to just sit on a throne—even though you do look pretty! And He didn't make you to just play all day or to be waited on by a royal staff.

So why did God make you? To do good works your whole life through. But that doesn't mean you won't have any fun. God's work is never dull or boring!

God's work is caring for friends and sharing what you have. It's singing sweet songs of praise. It's telling younger children the stories of Noah and how Queen Esther saved her people. It's smiling and being kind, giving, and forgiving. God's work is simply loving others the way He loves you.

Good-Night Giggles and Grace

You can learn to tell Bible stories to others. Line up Teddy and your other stuffed animals on your bed. Pick out your favorite Bible story and practice telling it to all your little "listeners" as well as Mom and Dad.

Dear Lord, I've got a job to do,
So this is now my prayer:
I want to show my love for You
By helping people everywhere.
Amen.

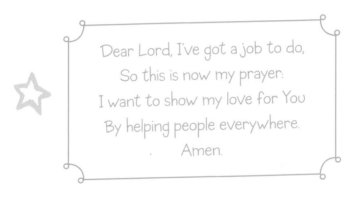

How to Sparkle Like the Sun

Depend on the Lord. Trust him, and he will take care of you. Then your goodness will shine like the sun. Your fairness will shine like the noonday sun.
—Psalm 37:5–6

Do you like things that sparkle and shine? Most princesses do! Twinkling tiaras, glittering gowns, and sparkly shoes—those are the things that make little princesses smile and say, *"Ooohhh!"*

But did you know that God likes sparkles too? It's true! But God likes His sparkles . . . *on you!* He doesn't use glitter or sequins or jewels to make you shine. So what does He use? Love and kindness. When you love God and then love others by being kind, it makes you sparkle—sparkle like sunshine.

God doesn't care what brand of clothes you wear because a heart filled with love and kindness is always in style.

Good-Night Giggles and Grace

Want to see how sparkles can light up the dark? Grab a flashlight and your most sparkly crown. Now turn off the lights. Shine your flashlight on your crown. See how the lights twinkle and dance? When you give others your love and kindness, you're like a sparkling light in a dark world.

Dear God,
You made the sun and moon so bright
And filled them with Your heavenly light.
So like the stars in heaven above,
I want to shine with Your pure love.
Amen.

God Calls Your Name

"Don't be afraid, because I have saved you. I have called you by name, and you are mine."
—Isaiah 43:1

Most moms and dads have some sort of special nickname for their little girls. Do you have any special names? Maybe it's Sweetie Pie, Punkin, or even Princess. Mom and Dad give you special names to show how much they love you.

Did you know that when you decide to follow God, He gives you a special name too? Can you guess why? Because He wants you to know how much He loves you. He calls you a child of God (1 John 3:1), a lamb (Isaiah 40:11), and precious (Isaiah 43:4). These names show that you belong to God. And when you belong to God, He promises to save you.

Good-Night Giggles and Grace

What are your special names? Ask your parents why they gave you these names. Make up special names for your mom and dad too!

Dear God,
Precious, child of God, and lamb—
That's what I'm called by the great I AM.
To follow You always is what I will choose.
I love that I belong to You.
Amen.

Prince Teddy

Lord Fluffy

Great Friends

Some people came, bringing a paralyzed man to Jesus.
Four of them were carrying the paralyzed man.
—Mark 2:3

Jesus was teaching inside a house, and everyone wanted to hear Him! The house was so full that not one more person could fit inside. People even filled up the doorway! But four friends just had to see Jesus. You see, they had another friend, and he couldn't walk. Jesus was his only hope.

The four friends saw the crowd, but they didn't give up. They went up—up on the roof! They cut a hole through the roof and lowered their friend down—right in front of Jesus! And Jesus healed their friend! Those four men did whatever it took to bring their friend to Jesus.

Will you do whatever it takes to bring your friends to Jesus? Will you risk being laughed at? Will you pray for them and invite them to church? That's what a true friend would do!

Good-Night Giggles and Grace

Read the whole story of these four friends in Mark 2:1–12. Then act out the story of these four friends with your mom or dad. Let your bed be the roof and Teddy be the man who couldn't walk. Careful when you lower Teddy down—don't let him fall!

Dear God,
Those four friends were pretty special,
And I want to be like them.
Help me bring *my* friends to Jesus,
And help others to meet Him.
Amen.

Time to Clean Up

Put these things out of your life: anger, bad
temper, doing or saying things to hurt others,
and using evil words when you talk.
—Colossians 3:8

The end of the day is a good time to clean up. Things are tidied away to get ready for a brand-new day.

The end of the day is also a good time to clean up your heart. Is there any yucky stuff that's collected in there throughout the day? Any bits of anger or fits of bad temper? Are there things you've said and done that you really shouldn't have? Those yucky things can stand between you and God, so it's time to clean them away. No, not with a vacuum or a feather duster—with a prayer! Ask God to forgive you and wash all those yucky things out of your heart.

When you ask God to forgive you, that's just what He'll do. Then your heart will sparkle like new!

Good-Night Giggles and Grace

Make your room *and* your heart sparkle. Throw those papers in the trash—and any mean thoughts too. Put away your toys, and make sure your temper is tidy. Put your dirty clothes in the hamper along with any ugly words. Then when it's time for bed, both your room and your heart will sparkle like new!

Dear God,
I will tidy up my room,
And I'll clean my heart inside.
Help me sweep out yucky thoughts
Like anger, ugly words, and pride.
Amen.

Obey Right Away!

When Joseph woke up, he did what the
Lord's angel had told him to do.
—Matthew 1:24

Just a minute! Not right now. I'll do it later!"

Is that what you say when Mom or Dad asks you to do something? It's not always fun to stop playing and go clean your room. Or run errands with Mom. Or get ready for bed. But that's what God wants you to do.

Before Jesus was even born, God sent His angel to speak to Joseph in a dream. The angel told Joseph to take Mary as his wife because she was going to have God's Son. When Joseph woke up, he didn't wait. He didn't say, "In a minute." Joseph hurried to obey.

That's what God wants you to do too. When your mom and dad tell you to do something, God doesn't want you to wait. He doesn't want you to say, "In a minute." God wants you to hurry to obey.

Good-Night Giggles and Grace

How quickly can you obey? When Mom or Dad say it's bedtime, how fast can you wiggle into your jammies? Can you find Teddy speedy quick? Can you tuck the covers up under your chin—before Mom and Dad can count to ten?

Dear God,
Sometimes it's hard to
stop what I'm doing—
I'm having such fun as I play.
But Mom and Dad said,
"Time to get moving."
So help me to quickly obey.
Amen.

Star Puppy
Award

Doggy Day
School

God's Still Working on You

God began doing a good work in you. And
he will continue it until it is finished when
Jesus Christ comes again. I am sure of that.
—Philippians 1:6

Maybe you tried to help bake cookies, but somehow they came out like rocks. Maybe you tried to swing up high in the sky, but you fell to the ground with a most un-princess-like *plop!*

You may wish you could do everything perfectly the very first time, but it usually doesn't happen like that. Baking cookies takes practice, and so does swinging high. And there are other things that take practice too, like sharing and forgiving and being patient and kind.

So maybe you shouted, "No!" when you should have said, "Yes, ma'am." Or maybe you lost your temper, and now you're in a jam. Don't give up on yourself. Keep trying. Do your best. And if you feel like giving up, remember this one simple truth: God's still working on you.

Good-Night Giggles and Grace

Most things take practice to get them just right. So practice your princess poses with Mom tonight. Work on your curtsies, your waves, and your smiles. Keep practicing, and you'll have them down pat—it's as simple as that!

Dear God,
I tried my best but failed again.
I won't give up—just watch and see.
When things don't go quite as I plan,
I'll know You're still at work in me!
Amen.

When Your Heart Hurts

The Lord is close to the brokenhearted.
He saves those whose spirits have been crushed.
—Psalm 34:18

Sometimes hearts—even royal hearts—get hurt and broken. Now your tears are falling, and they won't seem to stop. Maybe it's a not-too-big thing—a lost toy or a fight with a friend. Or maybe it is a *very* big thing—someone you love is sick or hurt. But whether big or small, or somewhere in between, your heart is royally broken.

Jesus knows just how you're feeling. He's had His heart broken too. He's been alone. He's had His friends turn away. Because Jesus has been hurt too, He knows just what you need.

So say a prayer, let Jesus hold you close, and trust Him with everything.

Good-Night Giggles and Grace

Curl up in Dad's or Mom's lap. Feel how warm and safe and loved you are? Snuggle your head on their shoulders. Snuggle your arms and even your toes. With an Eskimo kiss, snuggle your nose. Rock and sway and sing a little song. Next time you are sad, remember that a prayer and a snuggle can help fix what's wrong.

Dear God,
When my heart is hurting and sad,
When others have made me feel so bad,
I choose to give all my hurts to You,
For You make my heart feel all brand-new.
Amen.

Thank God for Special People

I thank God every time I remember you.
—Philippians 1:3

It's easy to think of gifts as presents that you open. But gifts can be people too—the people in your life who love you and the people whom you love. And when those people help you learn more about God and how to love and serve Him, then they're the very best gifts of all!

Who are some of your favorite people? Your mom and dad? Neighbors or cousins? Other family or friends? Do they live near or far?

When you thank God for all the many blessings He has given you, don't forget to thank Him for all the wonderful people in your life too!

Good-Night Giggles and Grace

Ask Mom or Dad to help you get out a family picture album. Just look at all the wonderful people who love you! Talk about each of them—who they are and why they are important to you. Then say a prayer for all your family, and thank God each time you remember them!

> Thank You, God, for uncles and aunts,
> My family and neighbors too.
> Thank You, God, for all the people
> Who teach me to follow You.
> Amen.

God Is Always Listening

*"If two or three people come together in
my name, I am there with them."*
—Matthew 18:20

When you pray, you are never alone. Your heavenly Father always comes to listen to you, His little princess.

But when you pray with others, that is a special time too because God comes to join all of you.

So gather with your mom and dad, and say a prayer for your family. As you go out to play with friends, hold hands and ask God to bless your time together. If you see someone who's hurt or in need, ask if you can say a prayer—and then go ahead and do it right there.

Don't worry about having exactly the right words to say. God's right there with you, and He knows all about it anyway.

94

Good-Night Giggles and Grace

Cut out a large red heart. As you say your good-night prayer with Mom or Dad, hold hands and make a circle. Place the heart in the middle to help you remember that God is right there, listening to your prayer.

Dear Father,
I pray that Your name will be kept holy,
And I pray that Your will be done.
Forgive my sins as I forgive others.
Protect me from the Evil One.
Amen.

What Can You Give?

*Jesus . . . said, "I tell you the truth. This
poor widow gave only two small coins. But
she really gave more than all those rich
people. The rich have plenty; they gave
only what they did not need. This woman
is very poor. But she gave all she had."*
—Mark 12:43–44

Maybe you're thinking, *I'm only a little princess, what
can I do?*

Oh, sweet princess, there's so much you can
do—if you give your heart to God! When you let His love
fill you up inside, it will find all kinds of ways to spill
out! You see, your gifts aren't just gifts of money, and
they don't have to be gifts of great size. A smile, a hug,
a little bit of your time, and a willing heart—that's what
God asks you to give.

It isn't the *size* of your gift that matters, it's just the
fact that you give!

Good-Night Giggles and Grace

The coins the widow gave might have been much like pennies. Start a collection of pennies. Each time you drop a penny in your collection, say this rhyme:

> Two pennies in my hand doesn't seem like much.
> But what could two pennies do with my Father's touch?

Then watch carefully for something God wants you to do with your pennies!

> Dear God,
> I want to help, but what can I do?
> I'm small, and I don't have a lot.
> Help me to remember each day
> You'll do miracles with what I've got.
> Amen.

God Can Do Anything!

Jesus looked straight at them and said,
"This is something that men cannot do. But
God can do it. God can do all things."
—Mark 10:27

Some things seem impossible—and for us they really are. But nothing is impossible for God and His Son. Just think of all the things they've done!

God made the world and everything in it. He made the moon, the sun, and the stars. He parted rivers, and He parted seas. Then Jesus came, and He helped so many people. He healed the sick and raised the dead with just a word. He helped the blind to see and the lepers to be healed. And those who couldn't walk? Jesus lifted them up to run!

God can do anything . . . well . . . almost anything. There are two things that God cannot do. He cannot lie, and He cannot break a promise (Numbers 23:19). So when God says He loves you and will take care of you—that's definitely something He can do!

Good-Night Giggles and Grace

Use your imagination to think of some of the many, many things that God can do. *Can God lift a mountain?* Of course He can—He's stronger than any man! *Can God go to Mars?* He doesn't even need a rocket because He made Mars! *Can God catch a whale?* I'm sure He only needs one hand!

Dear God,
Nothing is impossible for You or for Your Son.
I just have to remember all the
things that You have done.
You're the One who made the mountains
and the One who parted seas.
Thank You, God, that You are also
the One who cares for me.
Amen.

Jesus Is Coming!

The followers brought the colt to Jesus. They put their coats on the colt, and Jesus sat on it. Many people spread their coats on the road. Others cut branches in the fields and spread the branches on the road. Some of the people were walking ahead of Jesus. Others were following him. All of them were shouting, "Praise God! God bless the One who comes in the name of the Lord!"
—Mark 11:7–9

Jesus is the King of Kings and the Lord of Lords (Revelation 19:16). But when Jesus rode into Jerusalem for the last time, He didn't come in a royal chariot pulled by gleaming white horses. No golden trumpets announced His arrival. He could have had all these things, but He didn't.

Instead, Jesus rode humbly into Jerusalem on the back of a donkey's colt. Jesus didn't try to show everyone that He was better than they were. He came to serve and to love, and He hopes you'll follow His example and choose to be humble too.

Good-Night Giggles and Grace

Have a royal parade of your own! Make a path of blankets on the floor, and have Daddy give you a pony ride to bed. Be sure to practice your best princess wave as you ride!

Jesus, You'll come again someday.
I'll be ready when You do.
I want to march in the royal parade
And live in heaven with You!
Amen.

I Want, I Want, I Want

Then Jesus said to them, "Be careful and guard
against all kinds of greed. A man's life is not
measured by the many things he owns."
—Luke 12:15

want it now! That's mine! Give it to me!"

Those are some royally *un-royal* words! But have you ever said them? Most people have at one time or another—even daughters of the King. Why? Because it's so easy to be selfish and greedy. You don't really even have to try; it just comes naturally. But that doesn't make it right.

It's hard to say no to yourself. Some princesses have even been known to throw a fit to get what they want. Oh my! I'm sure that would never be you!

It's okay to want candy and toys and just stuff. And it's okay to have them. But a daughter of the King always remembers this: it's what fills your heart—not what fills your room—that makes you really royal!

Good-Night Giggles and Grace

Royal fits are the pits, and they make you look silly too! Don't believe it? Ask Mom or Dad to throw a temper tantrum. Don't they look silly? Next time you're tempted to throw a royal fit, remember you're a princess of the King—and you just don't do such things!

Dear God,
"I want, I want, I want it now!"
Did I really say that today?
I'm sorry I was selfish, Lord.
I'll try harder to obey.
Amen.

The Armor of God

*Wear God's armor so that you can
fight against the devil's evil tricks.*
—Ephesians 6:11

Every day is a battle. Not a battle of knives and swords, but a battle of good versus evil. A fight to do what is right. And although it's true you are a princess of the King, you are one of His mighty warriors too!

Like all good warriors, you need to put on your armor. But God's armor is a little different. It's not made of steel; it's made of faith. And you don't strap it on; you pray it on.

First, wrap the truth of God's Word around you like a belt. Next, protect your heart by trying to live right. Wear the good news about Jesus like shoes that help you stand strong. Your faith is your shield, and God protects your thoughts like a helmet. And your sword? That's the Bible! It fights the evil one's lies. Now you're ready to do battle for the King!

Good-Night Giggles and Grace

Dress up Teddy in the armor of God. Pray each piece onto him and yourself. (Belt—*Help me trust the truth of your Word*; shirt—*Help me live right*; shoes—*Help me share Jesus with others*; hat—*Protect my thoughts*; shield—*Protect me from the devil's lies*; sword—*Help me use Your Word to stop the enemy*.)

Dear God,
That sneaky old devil is after my heart,
So I'll get ready and do my part.
I'll pray Your protection over me—
Your mighty princess is what I'll be!
Amen.

Watch Those Words!

Do not be bitter or angry or mad. Never shout angrily or say things to hurt others. Never do anything evil.
—Ephesians 4:31

I t happens—even to daughters of the King. You get angry. You get mad. You stomp your foot, and your face turns red. And then you say . . . that thing you know you shouldn't say. You call names and throw around hurtful words.

Stop! Freeze! Take a deep breath!

It's okay to get mad, and it's okay to get angry. But don't let your anger make you mess up. Calling names and shouting hurtful words is a sin—and you need to say you're sorry, both to that person and to God. The next time you get angry, try this instead. Take a deep breath and count to ten. Then do what Jesus would do: be kind and loving and forgive each other just as God forgives you (Ephesians 4:32).

Good-Night Giggles and Grace

Practice saying nice names by adding some special words to everyone's name. For example: Marvelous Mommy, Darling Daddy, Lovable Lauren, Kind Kaler, and Groovy Grandpa!

Dear God,
Oh, God, I'm very sorry.
I said angry things again.
Please forgive my unkind words,
And help me tomorrow, amen.

God Will Take Care of You

"Look at the birds in the air. They don't plant or harvest or store food in barns. But your heavenly Father feeds the birds. And you know that you are worth much more than the birds."
—Matthew 6:26–27

D o you ever worry? Most people do once in a while—even God's little princesses. Jesus knew that His children would worry sometimes. That's why He tells us about the birds.

Birds don't go to work or have money, yet God gives them trees to live in and food to eat. Not a single little bird falls to the ground without God knowing (Matthew 10:29).

What does that mean for you? Just as God watches over the birds, He'll watch over *you* and give *you* what you need. And although you may not see Him, God is always with you.

So don't worry, sweet princess . . . you are worth much more than birds, and God will take care of you.

Good-Night Giggles and Grace

God takes care of the birds, but you can help too. Sprinkle some birdseed or bread crumbs on the sidewalk, your steps, or windowsill before you go to sleep. In the morning, see if the birds have found your gift!

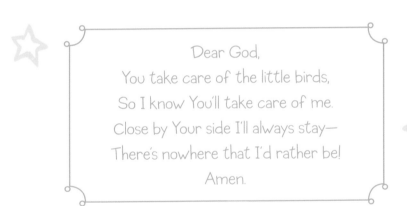

Dear God,
You take care of the little birds,
So I know You'll take care of me.
Close by Your side I'll always stay—
There's nowhere that I'd rather be!
Amen.

Rain and Sun and Snow

"Can you bring out the stars out at the right times? . . .
Can you shout an order to the clouds? . . .
Can you send lightning bolts on their way?"
—Job 38:32, 34–35

People have figured out how to do lots of things. We can fly around the world in jet airplanes. We can rocket ourselves to the moon. We can speed around in cars and can even send a ship to Mars!

But there are some things people just can't do. We can't make a snowflake. We can't fill the clouds with rain. We can't tell the storm clouds which way to go or tell the lightning where to strike. We can't tell the sun when to shine or show the wind where to blow. There's only One who can do all these things and so many, many more. He's the Lord of heaven and earth, and He's the Lord who loves you so!

Good-Night Giggles and Grace

What kind of weather did God give you today? Sunny? Cloudy? Pretend that God gave you a chance to control the weather for one day. What would it be like? Maybe you could make it rain flowers!

Lord, You shape the raindrops.
You know where the snow is stored.
The wind blows 'cause You tell it to.
You are amazing, Lord!
Amen.

God Is *Sooo* Big!

Who has measured the oceans
in the palm of his hand?
Who has used his hand to measure the sky?
Who has used a bowl to measure
all the dust of the earth?
Who has used scales to weigh
the mountains and hills?
—Isaiah 40:12

God is *sooo* big that He can measure the oceans and the sky. He knows how much dust is in the earth. And He can even weigh the mountains. Only God can do those things!

God is *sooo* big that you might wonder if He's too big to notice you. But that's simply not true! God knows every thought that you think and word that you speak. He sees every tear and knows each fear. He watches over you night and day. Yes, the God who can measure the oceans *is* amazing, and He thinks you're pretty amazing too!

Good-Night Giggles and Grace

Gather some measuring cups and spoons from the kitchen. As you snuggle down to sleep, imagine some of the ways God might measure His creation? How many spoonfuls of yellow are in a buttercup? How many scoops of water fill the ocean? How many cups of twinkle do you need to make the stars shine?

Dear God,
You hung the stars up in the sky.
You made the fish and birds that fly.
You made every single thing I see,
And still You choose to think of me.
Amen.

Please Forgive Me

*Be kind and loving to each other. Forgive each
other just as God forgave you in Christ.*
—Ephesians 4:32

Well, you did it. You messed up. You did what you knew you shouldn't do. You said those words you knew you shouldn't say. And now you're in trouble. *Big trouble!*

Even princesses can't always be perfect. Practically perfect, perhaps. But not perfectly perfect!

So what should a princess do when she messes up? Well, God knew that even His princesses would make mistakes and bad choices sometimes. That's why He gave you a way to make things right. First, you say you're sorry—both to God and to the person you hurt or disobeyed. Then you ask them both to forgive you, and try very hard not to make that same mistake again.

God asks only one thing in return: the next time that someone hurts you, you need to forgive that person too!

Good-Night Giggles and Grace

When you ask God to forgive you, He will wash you "whiter than snow" (Psalm 51:7). Cut a paper snowflake out of white paper. Hang it on your wall or door to remind you that when you mess up, God can make your heart whiter than snow!

Dear God,
I really messed up big this time,
And Mom said, "That's enough!"
I'm sorry. Please forgive me, Lord.
This growing up is tough!
Amen.

Tell All About It!

"If anyone stands before others and says that he believes in me, then I will say that he belongs to me. I will say this before the angels of God."
—Luke 12:8

What do you do when you have good news? You share it, of course! Well, Jesus is the very best news of all, so what should you do?

Jesus is God's own Son. He came to earth as a tiny baby and grew up just like you. He had brothers and sisters and chores to do. When He was all grown up, Jesus taught everyone who would listen all about God and how to get to heaven. He died on the cross to take away our sins, but then—and this is the greatest news of all—He rose from the grave. He defeated death so we can too.

And if you share the good news of Jesus with your friends, and they love Him too, the angels in heaven throw a big party that started with you!

Good-Night Giggles and Grace

Have Mom or Dad pretend to be a reporter. They could even use your hairbrush for a microphone. Let them interview you as you tell them about the greatest news of all—Jesus! If you have a video camera, you could even tape it and share it with family and friends.

Lord,
I've got some really good news,
And that good news is You.
I've got to tell the whole wide world
That Your promises are true!
Amen.

Good News!

Made in God's Image

God created human beings in his image.
In the image of God he created them.
He created them male and female.
—Genesis 1:27

Who do you look like? Do you look like your mom? Or do you look more like your dad? Do you have your grandfather's hair or your nana's eyes? Most people look a little bit like someone in their family.

But do you know who else you look like? God. Yes, it's true! You look like God because He created you in His image. That means He made you to look like Him. Oh, it's not that you have God's nose or His eyes, and you're definitely not as tall as He is! But all the good things you do—like being kind, sharing with others, smiling, and waiting your turn—those things come from God. And every time you do something good, you show that you're part of God's family—because you look just like Him!

Good-Night Giggles and Grace

Grab a mirror and take a peek at your royal reflection! Are there ways that you look like your mom? Are there ways that you look like your dad? Are some parts of you wonderfully and uniquely all you? Now, how about your heavenly Father—what are some ways you look like Him?

Dear God,
When I look in the mirror,
I hope to see
Your goodness and Your kindness
Smiling back at me!
Amen.

Run to God

*I love you, Lord. You are my strength. The Lord
is my rock, my protection, my Savior. My God
is my rock. I can run to him for safety. He is my
shield and my saving strength, my high tower.*
—Psalm 18:1–2

Some days it just seems that everything goes wrong! First, you stub your toe getting out of bed. And things only get worse from there! You spill your milk at breakfast, your best friend won't speak to you, and your puppy chews up your shoe! Then you're so angry that you smart off to your mom—now you're *really* having a bad day!

What should a princess do when everything seems to go wrong?

Run to God! Pray to Him, and tell Him all your troubles. God promises that when you run to Him, He will surround you with His love and comfort and protection like a castle tower! (But you still should say sorry to Mom!)

Good-Night Giggles and Grace

Turn your bed into a fortress! Pile up pillows and blankets and stuffed animals. Then grab Teddy and snuggle down inside. Just as your fortress of pillows surrounds you, God's love does too.

Dear God,
You are my castle where I hide.
I'm safe when I am by Your side.
I'll run to You when things get rough.
For You, no problem is too tough.
Amen.

What to Wear?

We should wear faith and love to protect us. And
the hope of salvation should be our helmet.
—1 Thessalonians 5:8

What to wear, what to wear? The purple one or the pink? Or maybe the blue one with yellow buttons? Should you wear fancy shoes or shoes made to run? Will it be a crown or a ribbon today? Deciding what to wear can be fun because there are so many choices to make!

But there's one part of your outfit that should never change whether you're headed to the park or to the ball. It's the part that you wear in your heart, and it's the most important part of all. Your heart should always wear love for God and faith in Him. That faith and love are what make you sparkle from within.

So whether you wear a T-shirt and jeans or a tiara with gloves, make sure your heart is dressed in love.

Good-Night Giggles and Grace

God says that you should wear faith and love wrapped around you—much like a robe. Borrow a robe from your mom or dad for the night. Pretend it is your faith in God and His love. Wrap it all around you—warm and snug. Then curl up and rest in His love.

Dear God,
Sometimes I love sparkly dresses
and shoes that shine.
Sometimes just jeans and a
T-shirt of mine.
But my favoritest thing of all to wear
Is Your love wrapped around me everywhere.
Amen.

God Carries You

The Lord takes care of his people like a shepherd.
He gathers the people like lambs in his arms.
He carries them close to him.
—Isaiah 40:11

Think of all the different people who love you and help take care of you—Mom and Dad and grandparents too. Maybe uncles and aunts, teachers and friends. So many people love and care for you.

But there's One who loves you even more than Mom and Dad do. It's hard to believe, but it's true! He is God, and He sent His own Son to save you. He watches over you day and night, just as a shepherd watches over his sheep. And when you are hurting or just plain tired, God scoops you up and carries you close to His heart. You may not see or feel Him, but He is always there—loving and caring for you.

And guess what? He loves your mom and dad that much too!

Good-Night Giggles and Grace

Have Mom or Dad carry you to bed while you both sing this song (to the tune of "Mary Had a Little Lamb"):

God loves you, His little lamb, little lamb, little lamb.
God loves you, His little lamb. Yes, He loves you so.

Lord, I am Your little lamb.
That's all I want to be.
Carry me close to Your heart—
Someday Your face I'll see!
Amen.

God Knows Everything!

*"Yes, God even knows how many
hairs you have on your head."*
—Luke 12:7

God knows everything—*absolutely everything!*

Just think of a question, any question at all—God knows the answer. He even knows what question you are going to ask *before* you ask it!

God is smarter than the smartest scientist. And He's greater than the most gifted genius.

God knows how many grains of sand are on the beach. He knows how many stars light the sky. He teaches the sparrows to fly and the lions to roar. He even knows the recipes for making snow and bright rainbows.

But the very best news of all is what God knows about you. He knows your hopes and dreams, and He knows just what you need. He knows you inside and out, top to bottom. He even knows how many freckles are on your nose!

126

Good-Night Giggles and Grace

Think of some questions you'd like to ask God. They can be serious, like, *Why did You send Jesus to save us?* or *How can I be more like Jesus?*

Or they can even be a little bit silly, like, *How many teeth does a hippo have? Where does the rainbow end?* or *How many hairs are on my head?*

Dear Lord,
You know every hair on my head
And the number of stars in the sky.
Thank You for being a God I can ask
Who, what, where, when, and why!
Amen.

God Made You Special

*Each of you received a spiritual gift. God
has shown you his grace in giving you
different gifts. . . . So be good servants
and use your gifts to serve each other.*
—1 Peter 4:10

It's easy to look around you and see all that others can do. *She* can swing higher. *She* can twirl faster. *He* can kick a ball farther.

But it's not always so easy to see the things that *you* can do. God doesn't want you to compare yourself to others. He made you special in your own wonderful way. God has given you a gift, but you may still be figuring it out. It might be singing or praising. Maybe it's writing or drawing. Or perhaps you're gifted at teaching or cheering others up. But no matter what your gift may be, remember that it came from God—so you know it must be great!

Good-Night Giggles and Grace

Are there some silly things only you can do? Can you rub your head while you pat your tummy? Can you do it while spinning around? Can you cross your eyes? Can you roll up your tongue when you stick it out? Can you wiggle your ears all around? What silly things can you do?

Dear God,
What gift did You give me?
Will I paint or teach or sing?
No matter what I'm good at,
I'll praise You for everything!
Amen.

How Can I Share Jesus?

*Jesus said, "Go home to your family and friends.
Tell them how much the Lord has done for
you and how he has had mercy on you."*
—Mark 5:19

Some things are hard to share, like favorite toys and chocolate chip cookies. But there's one thing you should always *want* to share—Jesus.

But I'm only a little princess, you might say, *how can I share Jesus?* Well, sharing Jesus isn't just about using big, fancy words or doing great deeds. Just tell others how much Jesus loves you, and then show that love in everything you do.

When you are loving and kind, that tells others that Jesus is on your mind. When you are helpful, that says a mouthful! When your words are gentle and true, that shows that Jesus' love lives in you.

When it comes to sharing Jesus, it's not just what you say; it's what you do!

Good-Night Giggles and Grace

Think of all the different people in your family. Then think of a way to tell them about Jesus that begins with the same letter as that person's name. For example, deliver it to Daddy, mail it to Mom, bounce it to Bob, and e-mail it to Aunt Ellen!

Dear God,
I've got the greatest news of all—
How to get to heaven above!
Teach me how to tell the world
All about Your awesome love.
Amen.

Pray First

*Then the king said to me, "What do you
want?" First I prayed to the God of heaven.*
—Nehemiah 2:4

Nehemiah was a man who lived a very long time ago. One day the king asked him a question. Nehemiah needed to answer it just right, so what did he do? *First*, he prayed to God. *Then*, he answered the king.

And that's just what you should do too! Whenever you have something tough to do—or even something easy—say a little prayer to God first. Ask Him to guide what you say and what you do.

Need to make a difficult choice? Pray first! Need to say something that's hard to say? Pray first! Need to be brave or to stand up for what's right? Pray first!

The God who helped Nehemiah thousands of years ago is the same God who will help you today!

Good-Night Giggles and Grace

God hears all your prayers no matter where you are. (Nehemiah was in the king's dining room when he prayed!) So pray yourself into bed tonight. Thank God for your toys as you put them away. Pray for friends to smile at as you brush your teeth. Ask God to help you share His light as you turn off the light. Keep praying all the way to sleep!

Dear God,
Teach me to pray about all that I do.
Help me to bring every single thing to You.
Amen.

No Bullies Allowed

*Speak up for those who cannot speak
for themselves. Defend the rights of
all those who have nothing.*
—Proverbs 31:8

Some kids get picked on. It's just a terrible fact. Maybe they look different or talk different or come from a different place—but that doesn't make it right.

What should you do when you see someone being bullied or teased? It can be tempting to run away yourself or pretend you didn't see a thing. After all, what if that bully decides to start picking on you?

But God asks you to be brave. Stand up for the one who is being hurt. Don't be afraid to say that something is wrong—and don't be afraid to get a grownup's help, if you need it!

A true princess of God sits with the girl who's all alone at lunch. She shares her time with those who need a friend. And a true princess *even* prays for the one who is being mean.

Good-Night Giggles and Grace

It's hard to know what to do when you see someone being picked on, so practice ahead of time. Gather up Teddy and two of his friends. Pretend that one of them is picking on another. With Mom and Dad's help, practice what Teddy should say and do.

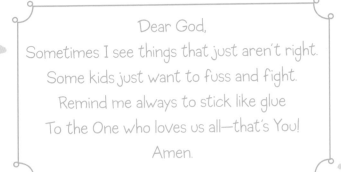

Dear God,
Sometimes I see things that just aren't right.
Some kids just want to fuss and fight.
Remind me always to stick like glue
To the One who loves us all—that's You!
Amen.

NO BULLIES

Thinking Good Thoughts

We capture every thought and make
it give up and obey Christ.
—2 Corinthians 10:5

Have you ever had a friend sneak up on you from behind? You didn't even know she was there until she said, "Surprise!"

Sometimes bad thoughts can be like that sneaky friend. Somehow they just slip right in and catch you by surprise. Maybe you are thinking how happy you are about your friend's new tiara, when suddenly this thought pops in: *It would look better on me!*

Or perhaps you are patiently waiting your turn on the slide, when suddenly you think, *I should jump line!* Or maybe you are on your way to help your mom when you think, *No! I want to play instead.*

Bad thoughts have a way of sneaking right in, even when you're trying to be good. It happens, and it's okay as long as you do this one thing: throw that bad thought right back out again!

Good-Night Giggles and Grace

Capturing bad thoughts is a lot like a cowgirl lassoing her horse. Grab a hoop or a ring—or just make one from some string—and pretend you're a cowgirl. (Don't worry—cowgirls wear sparkles too!) Can you lasso Teddy? Or Mom or Dad?

Dear God,
What was I thinking?
How did that thought get in?
I'm going to rope that nasty thought
And throw it in the bin!
Amen.

Don't Get Even

If someone does wrong to you, do not pay
him back by doing wrong to him.
—Romans 12:17

arah said some things to you that weren't nice! Brandon snatched your toy right out of your hand! Ellie pushed you off the swing!

When these things happen, what does it make you want to do? Say something back, snatch your toy away, push her off the swing too? Do you want to get that person back, get even, get revenge?

That's only natural—but God wants you to be *super-*natural! He doesn't want you to get even. When someone is unkind to you, guess what God wants you to do? He wants you to "try to do what everyone thinks is right," and "do your best to live in peace with everyone" (Romans 12:17–18). Living in peace might mean walking away. Or it might mean getting a grown-up to help. But it doesn't mean getting even!

Good-Night Giggles and Grace

Trying to "get even" isn't as easy as you might think! Take a piece of paper and—without folding it—tear it exactly in half. Are the pieces exactly even? No? Try tearing again to make them just right. Still not even? That's what happens when you try to get even with someone. It never quite comes out right because they often try to get you back!

Dear God,
When others aren't
so nice to me,
Help me to walk away.
Instead of trying to
get them back.
Help me to stop and pray,
Amen.

God So Loved . . . You

"For God loved the world so much that
he gave his only Son. God gave his Son
so that whoever believes in him may
not be lost, but have eternal life."
—John 3:16

What are some of the things you love most? Your mom and dad? Your Friends? Your dog? Your toys? Do you know what God loves most? You—and all the people of the world. How can you know that? Because His Bible tells you so.

In John 3:16, Jesus said that God loved the world's people so much that He gave up His own Son to save us. There is no greater love than that.

Because Jesus came, all your sins can be washed away. Because Jesus came, you can see heaven one day. And because Jesus came, you can truly be a princess—not just for pretend, but for real and forever, a princess of God the King.

Good-Night Giggles and Grace

Sing "Jesus Loves Me," but make it special just for you.
Instead of "me," say your own name. You can take turns
trying Mom's name and Dad's name too.

> Dear God,
> Lord, You love me, this I know
> Because Your Bible tells me so.
> To You I know that I belong.
> So thank You for Your love so strong.
> Amen.

It's Not All About You

Do not be interested only in your own life,
but be interested in the lives of others.
—Philippians 2:4

It's easy to get wrapped up in your own life—the games you play and the toys you want and the things you'd like to say. It's easy to forget that others have their own thoughts and things they would like to say and do.

But God wants you to be interested in others. How else will you know what they need? God gave you two ears but only one mouth for a reason, and that reason is this: you need to learn to listen to others and talk less— that's part of what makes you God's princess!

Good-Night Giggles and Grace

Polish your princess manners with a little practice. Have a bedtime "tea party" with some milk and cookies or crackers. Serve your mom and dad first, and ask them about their day. Make sure everyone gets a chance to have their say. And be sure to use your "please" and "thank you"—it's what polished princesses do!

Dear God,
Lots of people live in this world,
So everything's not about me.
Help me to reach out to others,
Just as You have reached down to me.
Amen.

God Helps Before You Even Ask

"I will provide for their needs before they ask. I will help them while they are still asking for help."
—Isaiah 65:24

God knows your thoughts, and He knows what's in your heart. He knows just what you will say before the words ever come out. And God also knows what you need before you pray about it. In fact, He promises to start helping *before* you even ask!

When God sees one of His children in need, He goes to work. He hopes that you will too! How? If you see something that needs to be done or someone who needs to be helped, don't wait to be asked. Just go ahead and do it! Take out the trash, and pick up that dropped spoon. Give your mom a hand with the groceries.

See how many things you can do before you're even asked.

Good-Night Giggles and Grace

Most of the time people help *after* they are asked, but sometimes God does the opposite—He helps *before*. Play a game of opposites. Have your mom or dad say a word (like *before, behind, under, hot, dark, soft,* and so on). Then you say the opposite.

Dear God,
You give me everything I need—
Sometimes before I even ask.
Show me what I can do today.
Who can I help out with a task?
Amen.

Shine Like a Star

You are living with crooked and mean
people all around you. Among them you
shine like stars in the dark world.
—Philippians 2:15

I n this world, there is darkness. Not just the kind of darkness you see at night, but a darkness *inside* some people. It can make them selfish, greedy, unhappy, and unkind.

The only way to get rid of darkness at night is to turn on the light, right? Well, the only way to get rid of darkness inside people is with light. But how? By showing them *your* light. Your light is your love for God. It shines when you are gentle and good and kind. It shines when you share and when you forgive.

Try to live in a way that people know you love Jesus, even if you don't say His name. When you let Jesus' love guide what you do, your own light shines bright—brighter than any star.

Good-Night Giggles and Grace

Shine your light in bed tonight—your flashlight, that is. Play a kind of flashlight tag on the wall with Mom and Dad. Each of you should have your own flashlight. Turn off the lights, and turn on your flashlights. See if you can "tag" Mom's light on the wall. How about Dad's? Don't let them tag yours!

Dear God,
I want to be a light
And shine in this world for You.
Let my love be oh so bright
So Your love will come shining through.
Amen.

Never Too Tired to Do Good

Never become tired of doing good.
—2 Thessalonians 3:13

Have you ever done something so many times that you just can't stand to do it even once more? Maybe you've turned cartwheels until your legs are all wobbly. Maybe you've twirled until the whole world is spinning round! Maybe you've played Go Fish until you're all fished out!

Or maybe you've just been a royally wonderful princess all day long, and it's time for your beauty rest!

There's only one thing God asks that you never get tired of doing and that you never be too tired to do. What is it? *Doing good.*

Never get tired of smiling or showing others that you care. Lend a helping hand—no matter how many times you have before. Never be too tired to give a hug or say a prayer. Try to share a little goodness every day and everywhere.

148

Good-Night Giggles and Grace

Yawning is a funny thing—it just has to be shared. If one person yawns, soon everyone else will be yawning too—it's true. Try it with your mom and dad. First, ask Mom or Dad to pretend to yawn. How long can you keep from yawning?

Dear God,
At times I do get tired
of always being good,
Of trying to do everything
that I know I should.
So help me, please, to rest well
all throughout the night
And then wake up to serve You,
Lord, with all my might!
Amen.

We Are All Important

*Do not be proud, but make friends
with those who seem unimportant.
Do not think how smart you are.*
—Romans 12:16

A re there people you don't see—or at least that you pretend not to see? Maybe it's the little boy next door who has trouble talking. Or the lady at church who squeezes your cheeks. Or maybe it's the little girl who walks with a brace—the girl everyone pretends isn't there.

They're not invisible, but people often pretend they are. Do you? Are there some people you ignore because you don't think they matter as much?

If you ever start to feel too royally regal for anyone else, think about Jesus. Who did Jesus hang out with? The rich and famous? No! The poor, the sick, and the sinners.

When you start to feel too good for someone else, remember that the King of the universe never felt too important to save you.

Good-Night Giggles and Grace

For just a few minutes, have Mom and Dad pretend you are invisible. As you get ready for bed, they might wonder why the water in the sink is running or whose pj's are waiting on the bed. Although it may seem a little silly as a bedtime game, it would get awfully lonely after a while. Pray and ask God if there's someone you need to "see" tomorrow.

Dear God,
There are so many people around me,
But which ones do I really see?
Help me see those who have been forgotten
And be who You need me to be.

Amen.

Jesus Stays the Same

Jesus Christ is the same yesterday,
today, and forever.
—Hebrews 13:8

Not many things always stay the same—not even princesses. As you grow up, you learn new things. And as you learn, you change the way you act and the way you think. You use new words and have new thoughts. The toys you played with when you were two probably no longer interest you. Even the friends you play with may change.

But Jesus *always* stays the same. The things that He said and believed in the days of the Bible are the same things He says and believes today, and they'll be the same tomorrow. That means His promises are always the same too. So the promise He made to His disciples—the promise to never leave (Matthew 28:20)—is the same promise He makes to you. And when He promised to make a room for them in heaven (John 14:2), He promises a room for you too!

Good-Night Giggles and Grace

Jesus never changes, but you certainly do! Take a look at some pictures of you, starting when you were a baby. See how much you've changed and grown! If Mom and Dad have their baby pictures, take a look at them too. Do they look a little different to you?

Dear God,
I'm growing taller every day
And learning lots along the way.
I'm changing all the time—it's true,
But thankfully You never do!
Amen.

Listen!

Always be willing to listen and slow to speak.
—James 1:19

Most princesses like to chatter—after all, they have important things to say! But sometimes it's good just to listen and not say a word.

Sometimes a friend just needs someone to hear all about her troubles and her joys. Sometimes Mom and Dad need you to listen—especially when it's time to put away toys! And it's important to listen to teachers because they have so much to teach you.

But the most important person to listen to is Jesus. You should *always* listen to Him. *But Jesus doesn't talk to me!* you might say. Oh, but He does—just in a different way. He talks to you through the words of the Bible and through those who teach you about Him. And when you stop to pray, remember to spend some time just listening. That's when He'll whisper His words from the Bible straight to your heart.

154

Good-Night Giggles and Grace

How well do you listen? Play a game of "Simon Says, 'Let's Get Ready for Bed!'" Have Mom or Dad call out all the different things you need to do to get ready for bed. But listen carefully and only obey when Simon says!

Dear God,
Sometimes I need to be still and quiet
And listen just to You.
So now I'll sit for a moment or two—
Listen is what I'll do.
(Sit quietly and just listen to God for a moment.)
Amen.

God Chooses . . . You!

*God has chosen you and made you his
holy people. He loves you. So always do
these things: Show mercy to others; be
kind, humble, gentle, and patient.*
—Colossians 3:12

So you didn't get picked to play the princess—even
though you were clearly perfect for the part! And
when it was time to choose teams, you were the
very last one to be chosen. And although you raised your
hand up high and waved it all around, the teacher didn't
ask you to be her helper today.

Cheer up, little princess. Try to smile and remember
this: There will be lots of plays, and lots of teams, and
lots of chances to help. But the choice that matters most
of all is the one you have to make yourself. That choice is
whether or not you choose God. Because, you know, He
always chooses you!

Good-Night Giggles and Grace

God has chosen you for His family! Sing "I'm in the Lord's Army"—princess style! Be sure to act it out as you sing.

I may never walk through a palace,
Ride in a carriage,
Sit on a throne,
I may never wear a real tiara,
But I'm in the King's family!

Dear God,
Sometimes life can be hard
When I don't get picked to play.
But I'm so glad I know one thing:
You choose me every day!
Amen.

God Makes You Strong

I can do all things through Christ
because he gives me strength.
—Philippians 4:13

God has great plans for your life. But God's plans for you don't start when you're all grown up—they start right now!

God might ask you to be a friend to someone who is lonely. He might ask you to give a toy to someone who doesn't have any. He might ask you to be kind or to be helpful or simply to listen to someone who is sad. Sometimes the things God asks you to do are easy and even fun. But sometimes He needs you to be strong and brave.

You never know what God might ask you to do, but there's one thing you can always count on: God will give you plenty of strength to do whatever He asks you to do!

Good-Night Giggles and Grace

Strike a pose, and show your muscles! Just like you exercise your body's muscles, you also need to exercise your "heart" muscles. "Heart" muscles are things like being kind, patient, thoughtful, and loving. As you drift off to sleep, plan something extra nice to do for someone when you wake. Let's get those "heart" muscles in shape!

Dear God,
Thank You for my muscles
That help me run and play.
Show me how to use them
To serve You every day!
Amen.

How to Be a Princess

*You are God's children whom he loves. So
try to be like God. Live a life of love. Love
other people just as Christ loved us.*
—Ephesians 5:1–2

B eing a princess isn't an easy thing. There are twirls to practice and curtsies to perfect. It takes work to get that princess wave just right. And all those things to remember—like poking out your pinkie when you sip your tea.

But being a princess of the King means even more. That's because:

P is for the princess who praises God her King.

R is for trying to do what's right.

I is for being made in the image of God.

N is for being nice, even when you'd rather not.

C is for courage to stand against wrong.

E is for enjoying all God's blessings.

S is for serving others.

S is for Savior, who loves you with all His might.

Good-Night Giggles and Grace

Can you add your own words to the "Princess" list? Words that tell about you? They can be silly or they can be serious—it's up to you!

Dear God,
I am a daughter of the most high King,
I'll do my best to be like You in everything.
I'm thankful that You give me love
and fill me with Your grace.
Teach me to live as Jesus lived until I see His face.
Amen.

☆ What Does Love Do? ☆

*My children, our love should not be only words
and talk. Our love must be true love. And
we should show that love by what we do.*
—1 John 3:18

Y ou can listen all day to the words of the Bible, and you can memorize verses by the dozen. But to truly obey God, you need to do what those words say.

God says be patient and be kind. Have you given that a try?

Love your enemies; that's what Jesus said. It's tough, but He wants you to do it!

Obey your parents. Yes, right away, so hop to it.

God doesn't want you just to listen but then do nothing (James 1:22). He wants you to put your love into action. When you love others, you show how much you love Him!

Good-Night Giggles and Grace

God wants you not only to know His words but also to do them. Act out ways you can show the fruit of the Spirit (Galatians 5:22–23) in your life—love, joy, peace, patience, kindness, goodness, faithfulness, gentleness, and self-control. Ready? Lights, camera . . . *action!*

Dear God,
Your love isn't just about words,
So help mine be more than words too—
To be gentle, patient, and kind.
And show just how much I love You!
Amen.

Oh-So-Sweet or Stomp Your Feet?

*I want to do the things that are good. But I do not
do them. I do not do the good things that I want
to do. I do the bad things that I do not want to do.*
—Romans 7:18–19

You know it's right. It's what a good princess would do. But you just don't want to! And suddenly you find yourself saying, "No! NO! *NO!*"

Perhaps your mom asks you to clean your room. Or your dad asks you to turn off the TV and set the table. Or a friend asks to share your favorite toy. You know you should, but . . . suddenly you're feeling grumpy and throwing a royal fit instead! Now big trouble is headed your way. What's a princess to do?

God understands it can be tough to be good and to always do what you should. So when you aren't very sweet, tell everyone, "Sorry!"—and then try even harder next time.

Good-Night Giggles and Grace

When the grumpies have got hold of you, try this little dance to feel brand new:

I don't want to yell and stomp my feet. (*stomp feet*)
I want to be kind and oh-so-sweet. (*smile sweetly*)
So when those grumpies start to hold on tight, (*hug yourself*)
I just stop and smile with all my might. (*smile sweetly again*)

Dear God,
Sometimes I don't want to be sweet.
I just want to yell and stomp my feet.
But this isn't how You want me to be.
Let others see Jesus shining through me.
Amen.

The Good Shepherd

"I am the good shepherd. I know my sheep, as the Father knows me. And my sheep know me, as I know the Father. I give my life for the sheep."
—John 10:14–15

A shepherd watches over his flock. He keeps each and every one of them safe—from the great big daddy sheep all the way down to the tiniest little lamb. The sheep know their shepherd and follow him. They trust the shepherd because he takes care of them.

Jesus says that He is like a shepherd, and we are His sheep. He keeps watch over each and every person in His flock—from the biggest, strongest dad and mom all the way down to the teeniest, tiniest baby. And He keeps watch over you—His sweet little princess lamb.

We trust Jesus our Shepherd because He takes care of us. Jesus even died to save us because He loves us so.

Good-Night Giggles and Grace

A good shepherd is very busy and doesn't let any of the flock get lost! Gather your royal flock of stuffed animals, and shepherd them into bed. But don't let any wander away—watch out for that Teddy trying to slip into the closet and that puppy hiding under the bed. Oh my! Is that a bunny hopping down the hall?

Dear God,
I am Your little lamb.
Teach me to follow You.
Please guide my feet and guard my heart
And keep me ever true.
Amen.

God Is *Sooo* Good

I will tell of your goodness. I will
praise you every day.
—Psalm 35:28

God is so good, and He is so good to you—His own beautiful little princess. Just think of all the gifts that He gives you every day. Families who love you and friends who hug you. Air to breathe and trees to climb. Sunshine and snow, wind and rain.

But do you know what the very best thing God ever gave you is? It's His Son! God gave up His only Son so that *you* could go to heaven and be His princess for all time. All you have to do is love Him and do what He teaches you in the Bible. Then one day you'll see Him in heaven. Yes, God is *sooo* good!

Good-Night Giggles and Grace

Sing a praise to God as you "hokey pokey" into bed!

I put my toes in. I take my toes out.
I put my toes in, and I wiggle 'em all about.
I know that God's the greatest. It makes me want to shout:
God's what it's all about!

Keep singing as you "hokey pokey" your toes, legs, arms, and whole self into bed!

God, You are so good to me.
I want to let You know.
I'm as thankful as I can be
Because You love me so!
Amen.

Thinking Heavenly Thoughts

Be very careful what you think.
Your thoughts run your life.
—Proverbs 4:23

Your thoughts can be filled with good things or bad, but they're always filled with something. And because the things you think about can quickly become the things you do, it's important to be careful what thoughts you let in there!

For example, if you think about saying that bad word, sooner or later it will slip out of your mouth. If you think about sassing your mom, chances are it will happen. And if you think about lying to get out of trouble, it becomes so much easier to do!

So what sort of thoughts *should* a princess think? This is what God says to you: "Think about the things that are good and worthy of praise. Think about the things that are true and honorable and right and pure and beautiful and respected" (Philippians 4:8).

That's the kind of thoughts a princess should think!

Good-Night Giggles and Grace

Some people say that a little bit of icky is okay. Let's see what you think. Ask Mom or Dad for a glass of water. All pure and clear, right? Now, add just one little drop of hot sauce. What does the water look like now? Do you want to drink it? Even a little icky thinking can mess up a whole day!

Dear God,
Help me to hear what You want me to hear,
To see what You want me to see.
Guide and protect my every thought,
For Your princess I always will be.
Amen.

Wanting What God Wants

*"The thing you should want most is God's
kingdom and doing what God wants."*
—Matthew 6:33

But I want to . . ."

Do you ever say those words? Maybe you say them when it's time to eat your vegetables—"But I want to eat dessert!" Or when it's time to come inside—"But I want to keep playing!" Or even when it's time to go to bed—"But I want to stay up late!"

Your parents tell you to do things—like eat your vegetables and get some rest—because they want what's best for you. In the same way, God wants what's best for you too. He wants you to learn to be a little more like Jesus every day. So He might ask you to share your toys, to spend some time helping others, or to pray for someone who has hurt your feelings.

Learning to put others first will help you be more like Jesus—and that's what God wants!

Good-Night Giggles and Grace

Not all wants are bad. Some are actually very good—like wanting to love God and to be helpful and kind. Other wants are fun or dreamy or even just plain silly! If you could do anything you want, what would you do? Would you flap your arms and zoom up to the moon? Eat ice cream for every meal? Swim with dolphins over the waves? Or teach your dog to sing?

God in heaven, You know what's best
In every single day.
Teach me tomorrow to follow Your heart
In every little way.
Amen.

Building with Love

Love builds up.
—1 Corinthians 8:1

id you know that a princess can be a builder? Yes, it's true! So gather up your tools, and join God's construction crew!

No, you won't need a hammer or nails or a saw. And you won't have to wear a construction hat at all—unless you want to, of course! So what are the tools that you will need? There's just one, really. Love. Yes, that's the tool you'll need.

But what can you build with love, you ask? A tree house? A bridge? Or a skyscraper tall? No, love builds things much more important than that—the most important things of all. Love builds families and friendships.

So how do you use this tool called love? Well, it's in the way you talk and the things you do. Say kind words. Share toys, smiles, and hugs. Help out whenever you can. Tell others all the things you like about them, and tell everyone about Jesus—He can build great friendships!

Good-Night Giggles and Grace

Even builders need their beauty rest! So build up a stack of snuggly pillows and your favorite stuffed animals. As you build, name some things you can do to show love to the people around you—hug a friend, call a shut-in, smile at everyone you meet.

Dear God,
I want to be a builder and work for You;
To build others up is what I want to do.
I don't need a hammer, a nail, or some gloves—
Just fill my heart, Lord, with Your love from above!
Amen.

Be Still

God says, "Be quiet and know that I am God."
—Psalm 46:10

I t isn't easy to be still, even for a princess. First, your nose starts to itch. Then your toes begin to twitch. Your tiara slips, and the next thing you know, you're doing flips!

Sometimes it's good to be wild and wiggly, but sometimes it's good to be quiet and still. When you're quiet, you can hear so many more things—like the wind that God made to whisper through the trees. And when you're still, you can see so many more things—like the way the stars twinkle in different colors or the way the sunset is different each day.

Sometimes we hear God speak in the roar of the wind and the rain. But sometimes God whispers and shows Himself to us through the quiet beauty of the world He has made. So take a little time each day to be still and quiet—and know God.

Good-Night Giggles and Grace

Bedtime is a time to be still, but sometimes wiggles get trapped inside! To get those wiggles out, start with your toes and wiggle them really well. Then move up to your legs, your tummy, arms, and fingers. Then give your whole body one last big wiggle. Now it's off to sleep—well, maybe just one more giggle!

Dear God,
You know how I love to run and shout,
But I want to learn what You're about.
Help me to listen in the quiet now.
As I say this prayer, to You I bow.
Amen.

Calling God

"You will call my name. You will come to me
and pray to me. And I will listen to you."
—Jeremiah 29:12

How do you talk to God? Do you call Him on the phone? Or send Him an e-mail? Or write Him a letter? Or do you just give a big shout? No—God isn't on the phone. He doesn't answer e-mails. And the mailman doesn't deliver all the way to heaven! Yes, you could shout, and God would hear you, but there's no need to be loud. All you really have to do to talk to God is pray!

That's God's wonderful promise to you. If you pray to God, He will listen. It's just that simple. No phone numbers to remember, no e-mail addresses to type, and no stamps to stick! God is never more than a prayer away.

Good-Night Giggles and Grace

You can't call God on the phone, but you can call God's family—and yours! Call Grandma or Grandpa or one of your favorite people. Then say a good-night prayer together.

Good night, God.
It's been a happy day.
Thank You, Lord,
For listening when I pray.
Amen.

Jesus Set an Example

*"I, your Lord and Teacher, have washed your
feet. So you also should wash each other's
feet. I did this as an example for you."*
—John 13:14–15

A princess shouldn't clear away dishes! Or give puppies a bath! Or wash stinky old feet! Or . . . should she?

Jesus was called the King of the Jews, but He didn't come to sit in a palace and order people around. He came to love and to serve and to save—and even to wash feet. *But why would Jesus wash feet?* you might wonder.

Jesus washed His disciples' feet as an example to them—and to you—of how we should love and care for each other. If Jesus, the Son of God and the King of all creation, wasn't too good to wash His disciples' feet, then there was nothing they were too good to do. And there's nothing you're too good to do either!

Good-Night Giggles and Grace

Of course, Mom's feet aren't stinky, but you can still pamper her toes. Paint Mom's toenails, and let her paint yours too. Maybe Mom will let you paint your dolly's toes!

Dear God,
Help me to be like Jesus,
Ready and willing to serve.
And showing others You love them
Because that is what You deserve.
Amen.

You're Just the Right Age

You are young, but do not let anyone treat you as if you were not important. Be an example to show the believers how they should live. Show them with your words, with the way you live, with your love, with your faith, and with your pure life.
—1 Timothy 4:12

You're not old enough to stay up really late or travel alone. You're too young to drive a car—you can't even ride your bike that far!

There are lots of things that you're just too young to do right now. But there are some things—really the most important things of all—that you're always just the right age for.

You're old enough to love God and to love others. You're old enough to smile and to say helpful, kind words. You're old enough to pray and to live as God wants you to each day. And when it comes to telling others about Jesus, well, you're just the right age!

Good-Night Giggles and Grace

You may not be old enough to do some things, but there are lots of things you *can* do. For every year of your age, name something you can do. For example, if you're five, name five fabulous things you can do—walk the dog, take out the trash, help carry in groceries, pick up your toys, and tie your own shoes!

Dear God,
There are some things I cannot do
But lots of things I can.
Show me the ways that I can serve—
No matter how old I am!
Amen.

God's Love Has No End

Your love is so great it reaches to the skies.
Your truth reaches to the clouds.
—Psalm 57:10

Most things have an ending. Stories do. Days and nights do. Even roads end sooner or later. But one thing does not end, not ever. That is God's love for you.

Imagine that God's love is like an invisible ribbon tied to your heart. God's love stretches from your heart all the way to the other side of the room. It stretches out the window, up past your roof, and into the sky. But it doesn't stop there! It stretches up past the clouds and reaches past the stars, and then it just keeps on going and going and going!

God's love has no end. He started loving you before you were even born. He loved you yesterday. He loves you today. And He will love you tomorrow. God's love for you will keep on going and going . . . forever.

Good-Night Giggles and Grace

God's love stretches up past the heavens, but how far can you stretch? Stretch up tall, as tall as you can! Now stretch down low, all the way to your toes. Stretch to one side and then the other—reach as far as you possibly can. Climb into bed and give one last big stretch. Now it's time to rest.

Oh, Lord, Your love reaches up so high,
Higher than even the birds can fly.
And I'm as grateful as I can be
That it also reaches down to me.
Amen.

You, Wonderful You

*Do not change yourselves to be
like the people of this world.*
—Romans 12:2

So you always seem to twirl left when you are supposed to whirl right. Or perhaps your favorite dress isn't as sparkly as everyone else's. Or when all the other kids start calling the new girl by not-so-nice names, you decide to stand by her side instead.

You only want to fit in, but you stick right out! And now the kids are whispering and giggling and throwing looks *your* way. What's a princess to do?

Should you change the way you twirl? Not for the world. Feel bad about your dress? No way! Just think how you're blessed. Join in the name-calling game? That would be a shame!

Sometimes it's hard to be different from everybody else, especially when others want you to do something you know is wrong. Don't change who you are just to try to fit in. Be who God wants you to be . . . and, darling, don't change a thing!

Good-Night Giggles and Grace

Play a game of bedtime dress-up. Borrow pajamas from Mom or a T-shirt from Dad. Add some slippers and fuzzy socks and a crazy scarf for your hair. Be sure to dress Mom and Dad up too. When you're all done, take a peek in the mirror. Then say in your very best royal voice, "Darling, I wouldn't change a thing!"

Dear God,
When I am feeling left out
And different and blue,
Help me to remember
I was wonderfully made by You!
Amen.

Why?

The Lord says, "Your thoughts are not like my thoughts. Your ways are not like my ways. Just as the heavens are higher than the earth, so are my ways higher than your ways. And my thoughts are higher than your thoughts."
—Isaiah 55:8–9

Why? Why do butterflies begin as caterpillars? Why do kangaroos hop? And why do elephants have such long noses?

Why are storms so scary? Why is the dark so . . . dark? Why do people get sick?

Why? Why? Why? You could fill an ocean with questions and still have more. Every little princess wants to know why. But there are some questions you'll never know the answer to.

God's way of thinking is so much more powerful than yours—or anyone's—that you just can't understand the way His thoughts work. You simply have to trust. Trust that God loves you and wants what's best for you. And that He has a reason for making kangaroos hop!

Good-Night Giggles and Grace

Do you have some questions for God? Like, *What really happened to the dinosaurs? Where does the rain come from? Why do ducks quack? And did You really have to make spiders?* Take turns wondering aloud with Mom or Dad. They probably have some questions too!

Dear God,
There are so many answers I'd like to know—
Where does wind come from?
How do You make snow?
But there is one answer I already know . . .
That Jesus is the answer, and He loves me so!
Amen.

Nothing Stops God's Love

Nothing now, nothing in the future . . . will ever be able to separate us from the love of God.
—Romans 8:38

When you choose to follow God, nothing can come between you and His love. Nope, not one single little thing!

Can a wall keep God away? No way! Can an army keep you apart? Nope, you're always in God's heart. Can the wind blow God's love away? Not even the wildest, windiest day!

There's no mistake you can make, no word you can say, no fit you can throw that will keep God from loving you. He loved you before you were born, He loves you now, and He will love you for all time.

When you choose to follow God, you become His daughter—a precious princess of the Great King. And nothing can keep Him from loving you—nope, not one single little thing!

Good-Night Giggles and Grace

Think of all the things that separate—things like fences and doors, locks and walls. Now think of a way God could get past each of those things, something that starts with the same letter. For example, God flies over the fence and dashes through the door. How many things can you think of?

> Dear God,
> Walls keep in, and walls keep out.
> Fences keep people apart.
> But I am grateful there'll never be
> A wall between You and my heart.
> Amen.

Love One Another

*Dear friends, we should love each other, because
love comes from God. The person who loves has
become God's child and knows God. Whoever does
not love does not know God, because God is love.*
—1 John 4:7–8

Love is more than hugs and kisses, and it's more than
something you feel. Love is something you *do*.

Sometimes it's calling friends and family who
live far away. It's baking cookies for a new neighbor. It's
taking flowers to someone who is sick.

And sometimes love is doing what's right—even when
you don't feel like it. It's cleaning your room because Mom
asked you to. It's giving up your allowance to help someone in need. It's spending Saturday morning helping Dad.

And sometimes love is listening and praying and
reading the Bible. It's singing praises and thanking
God for all His gifts.

No, love isn't just something you feel—it's something
you do. Oh, and sometimes . . . love is hugs and kisses too!

Good-Night Giggles and Grace

Think about all the different people you see. How can you show them God's love? How can you show love to your mom and dad? How about your neighbors and friends? The grocery store clerk or the lady at the library? How many different ways can you love this week?

Dear God,
Love one another, that's what we should do.
That's how others will learn about You.
Lord, You have loved me from the start,
Now, please help me to do my part.
Teach me to love as You love me,
With kindness and patience, unselfishly.
Amen.

Be Brave!

*"In this world you will have trouble. But
be brave! I have defeated the world!"*
—John 16:33

This world isn't perfect, not like heaven will be. In this world some things will be wonderful, but some things will be tough—even tougher than twirling on your tippy-top toes. And some things will be hard—even harder than eating your veggies. Some things will be sad—even sadder than a princess dress without any sparkles at all. And some things may even be a little scary—scarier than facing a dragon without your trusty sword!

But no matter what tough or hard, sad or scary thing you may have to face, there's one thing you must remember: be brave! Jesus has already defeated all the stuff of this world. He'll stand right by you and help you defeat it too!

194

Good-Night Giggles and Grace

Do you trust your mom and dad to catch you if you fall? Try this "trust fall": Stand with your back to your mom. Then let yourself fall backward as she catches you. Now try it with your dad. Moms and dads are there to catch you when you fall—and Jesus is too!

Dear God,
When things get tough or scary
And I'm feeling not-so brave,
Help me to remember—
You're by my side to save!
Amen.

✶ Trust God's Plans ✶

*All the days planned for me were written
in your book before I was one day old.*
—Psalm 139:16

D o you have plans for tomorrow? Is there a royal tea party to attend? What about next week? Is it time to polish your nails in princess pink? Is there a shopping trip on the royal calendar?

A busy princess probably has *some* plans, but do you know what you'll be doing next year? How about ten years from now? Or twenty? Or even fifty? You may not know, but God does! He planned out every day of your life—before you were even one day old!

And in Jeremiah 29:11, God says that His plans are for good, to give you hope and a future. What does that mean? It means God only wants the very best for you. *And* whenever you're facing a royally wretched problem, God already has the answer all figured out. Just trust Him and His perfect plan!

  196

Good-Night Giggles and Grace

Take a look at your ultrasound pictures (these are the pictures from when you were a baby inside your mom's tummy) or some pictures of when you were a tiny baby. Just imagine . . . God planned out your entire life before you were one day old! What might those plans be? As you snuggle in to sleep, pray that God will help you be the person He planned for you to be.

Dear God,
What will my life bring?
Lord, only You know.
But I'll trust You in everything
'Cause You love me so.
Amen.

God Sees Your Heart

*"God does not see the same way people
see. People look at the outside of a person,
but the Lord looks at the heart."*
—1 Samuel 16:7

How do you see? With your eyes, of course! Your eyes are amazing. They can see colors and shapes and the way things move. They can see in the sunshine and in the shadows. They can see things up close and things far away. But there are some things your eyes cannot see. They cannot see what someone is thinking or feeling.

But God can. His eyes see the outside of a person *and* the inside! That means God can see what you're thinking and feeling. If you look like a princess on the outside, but you think like a fire-breathing dragon on the inside, God will know! He doesn't care how you look or how fancy your clothes are.

So make sure you fill your mind with good thoughts and your heart with kindness. God is looking for a princess who will love and follow Him—inside and out.

Good-Night Giggles and Grace

God sees everything, but what can you see? Roll a piece of paper into a tube—like a spyglass. What do you see? Your books and toys, windows and door? Now pretend it's a special spyglass that lets you see *inside* things—just like God can. What's inside your toy box? Or Teddy's tummy? Or your heart?

Lord, You see everything there is to see—
Even the things hidden deep inside me.
Change my heart, and fill it with good.
Help me to think the sweet things I should.
Amen.

Serving God

Do not be lazy but work hard. Serve
the Lord with all your heart.
—Romans 12:11

But I'm a princess! A princess shouldn't have to . . . take out the trash, clean up her room, or give the puppy a bath!

Have you ever thought anything like that? Some jobs are kind of fun—like taking your puppy for a walk or feeding your goldfish. But some jobs are not so fun. You might even think that because you're a princess, you shouldn't have to work. But God says, "Don't be lazy!"

There's so much a princess can do! You can help your mom and dad around the house, you can help take care of a little brother or sister, and you can serve the Lord too. Dust the pews, sing songs to the babies, or pick flowers for Sunday bouquets.

Even a princess has to do her part. So serve the Lord with all your heart.

Good-Night Giggles and Grace

Your parents do so much for you! What can you do for them? Why not trade places tonight? Pick out clothes for them to wear tomorrow. Remind them to brush their teeth. Pretend to tuck them in instead.

Dear God,
When I'm working for You, I'm never bored.
There's just so much to do—
Give a helping hand, show people the Lord,
And teach them the Bible is true.
Amen.

God Loves to See You Smile

*Lord, you have made me happy by
what you have done. I will sing for joy
about what your hands have done.*
—Psalm 92:4

Just think of all the things in this world that make you happy—so happy you just want to sing! There are family and friends, special toys, princess slippers with extra sparkles, and, of course, ice cream! There are also snuggly puppies and bright rainbows, trees to climb and stars to count, icicles to chomp and puddles to stomp! The list could go on and on.

But do you know what all these things have in common? They are all gifts from God. God made many things just because you need them—air to breathe and water to drink. But some things God made just to make you smile. After all, God didn't have to make puppies so snuggly or rainbows so bright, but He did. Perhaps that's because God loves to see you smile!

Good-Night Giggles and Grace

As you climb into bed, sing a special good-night version of "If You're Happy and You Know It." For the first verse, sing, "If you're happy and you know it, yawn real big." For the second verse, sing "stretch up high." And for the third verse, sing "say good night." Sing a little bit softer with each new verse!

Lord, I'm happy and I know it—
It's because You've blessed me so.
I just need to sing about it—
'Cause the whole world ought to know!
Lord, I'm happy and I know it—
I just have to smile and sing
And twirl up on my toesies
Because, Lord, You are my King!
Amen.

Speaking Like a Princess

*Speak to each other with psalms, hymns,
and spiritual songs. Sing and make
music in your hearts to the Lord.*
—Ephesians 5:19

Did you know that princesses have their own special way of speaking? It's true! No, it's not just using a lot of fancy words, like *tiara* and *carriage* and *waltz*. And it's not just giving orders: *Fetch this! Get that! Serve me!*

No, a princess of God speaks with words of praise. That means you should try to find a way to please God with every word you say. What's your favorite Bible story? Tell your little brother. How did God make your teacher special? Let her know. How much do you love Jesus? Tell the world. Your beautiful words will be like music to everyone around you—and to God!

Good-Night Giggles and Grace

Lay your head on Mom's or Dad's chest. Listen closely—do you hear the heartbeat? What's it saying? Make up your own song to the "bom-bom" rhythm of the heartbeat. It might be something like this:

> I am a princess. Yes, it's true,
> But God is my heavenly King.
> He fills my heart with love and joy.
> He is my everything!

> Dear God,
> You fill my life with love.
> It's something I want to share.
> Help me to show the world
> How very much You care.
> You fill my heart with music.
> You fill my life with song.
> You are so very good to me.
> With You, I can't go wrong!
> Amen.

Jesus Never Leaves

"You can be sure that I will be with you always."
—Matthew 28:20

'll be right back!"

You probably hear that a lot, don't you? Maybe Mom is going to the grocery store, or Dad has to get something out of the garage. Moms and dads can only be in one place at a time. So sometimes they have to leave for a bit—but they'll be right back.

Jesus is different though. Jesus is God, and He can be everywhere—*all at the same time!* He's with you when you pray and when you go to church. But He's also at your tea party and your dance recital (and your brother's baseball game too). He's with you in the morning and at bedtime and at every time in between!

Jesus never says, "I'll be right back!" That's because He never leaves—not even for a moment. You may not see Him, but He's always there. You can be sure of that!

Good-Night Giggles and Grace

Your shadow is always with you. Sometimes you see it clearly; sometimes it's tiny and small; sometimes it's hiding and waiting to pop out. But it's always there, and it goes wherever you do. Every time you see your shadow, remember that Jesus is always with you too!

Dear God,
I look upon my shadow—
It dances on the wall
And helps me to remember
You never leave at all!
You're with me in the morning.
You're with me through the night.
You never leave in darkness
Or when it's shiny bright.
Shadows, shadows on the wall,
They help me to see.
You never, ever leave
Your little princess—me!
Amen.

How to Choose

You will teach me God's way to live.
Being with you will fill me with joy.
—Psalm 16:11

As a princess, you have lots of choices to make. Which tiara—the diamond or emerald? Which tutu—the pink one or the one with purple polka dots? Should you have a dress-up tea party with all your princess friends or make mud pies instead?

Then there are the days when you have to make really tough choices, but you still have to choose. When you knock over the lamp, do you lie or tell the truth? When your friend wants to play with your favorite doll, do you share? Do you use kind words or mean words; which do you choose?

It can be hard to make the right choice sometimes, but that's where God helps you out. His Word always teaches the right thing to do. Tell the truth, share, and be kind—you'll never go wrong when you keep God's Word in your mind.

Good-Night Giggles and Grace

As you grow up, you'll have to make a lot of important choices. Tonight, let's just choose your path to bed! Lay out a trail of socks for you to follow to bed—or ask Mom or Dad to do it. It might be a straight path or take lots of crazy turns—it's up to you to choose how you make it!

Dear God,
There are so many choices for me to make.
It can be hard to choose.
Fill my heart with Your holy Word,
So I'll always choose You!
Amen.

Mumble, Grumble, Grump

Do everything without complaining or arguing.
—Philippians 2:14

"Turn off the television. Pick up your toys. It's time to stop making quite so much noise!"

Do these words make you mumble? Or grumble? Or whine and complain? If they do . . . well . . . you might need to try again.

God asks His princesses—yes, you too—to do all things without complaining or arguing. Not some things. Not just the things you feel like doing. But *all* things.

Wow! That's tough. But with a little change in attitude, you can do it. Just try to make something fun of everything you have to do. *Need to sweep the kitchen?* Pretend you're sealing the castle door so bad guys can't come in. *Pick up your toys?* Pretend you're setting up a new toy store. *Play quietly?* Pretend you're a spy and can't get caught!

With a little practice and some imagination, you can change your mumbly grumblies into smiles, just like God wants you to!

Good-Night Giggles and Grace

Are you mumbly grumbly at bedtime? As you and Mom and Dad stomp your way to bed, try not to giggle as you say this grumbly rhyme (be sure to use your best grumbly voice):

Mumbly, grumbly, grump!
I'll stomp my feet, thump-thump,
And jump in bed with a bump.
Mumbly, grumbly, grump!

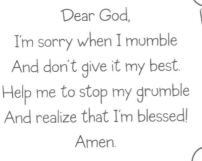

Dear God,
I'm sorry when I mumble
And don't give it my best.
Help me to stop my grumble
And realize that I'm blessed!
Amen.

Where Is God?

"You will search for me. And when you search
for me with all your heart, you will find me!"
—Jeremiah 29:13

Have you ever played hide-and-seek? Was there someone you searched and searched for but just couldn't find? Or maybe you were the one who found the very best hiding place, and no one could find you!

Hide-and-seek is a fun game, but it's not a game that God ever plays. God never hides from you—not even for fun. God *wants* to be found. And He promises that as soon as you start to look for Him, He will come running right to you!

So how do you look for God? That's easy! Just read His Bible and pray. Then God will come running to meet you—right away!

Good-Night Giggles and Grace

Have a game of bedtime hide-and-seek. But instead of hiding yourself, have Mom or Dad hide all the things you need to get ready for bed—like your toothbrush and toothpaste, pajamas, and Teddy. When you find all your good-night things, it's time for bed!

Dear God,
I don't have to look for You.
I know right where You are.
I just need to call Your name,
'Cause You're never very far.
Amen.

Amazing God

*You wear light like a robe. You stretch out
the skies like a tent. You build your room
above the clouds. You make the clouds your
chariot. You ride on the wings of the wind.*
—Psalm 104:2–3

God created all the heavens and all the earth. He created the light and the stars. He created the clouds and the wind. All of creation is His.

God wears the sunshine like a glittering robe. The stars are His tent, and the clouds are His chariot. He carved out the depths of the oceans with a word. Then He filled them with creatures large and small. He built the mountains up until they touched the sky. He made the birds that sing and the lions that roar.

The God who did all this and more is the same God who loves you—and He holds you up in His hand (Isaiah 41:10). Isn't He amazing?

Good-Night Giggles and Grace

God created everything—even the air that you breathe. You can't see it, but it's very real. Fill a balloon with air. You still can't see the air, but you *can* see how it fills the balloon. What are some other things God has made that you can't see? (Here's a hint: He made love and joy!)

Lord, You made everything I see.
You built up the mountains and dug out the seas.
But of all Your creation, my most favorite part
Is the love that You've placed right here in my heart.
Amen.

God Always Listens

The Lord listens when I pray to him.
—Psalm 4:3

What happens when God's little princess prays? God listens. Always. *Every single time.*

God doesn't just listen once in a while or only on Sundays or only at bedtime. God listens every time you pray. You can pray out loud, or you can pray without making any sound at all—God still hears each and every word.

You can pray in your bed or in the tub or at the kitchen table. You can pray in the morning and at night and at every time in between. Because no matter where you are or what time it is, God will always listen to you.

So before you snuggle up tight, have a little talk with God tonight!

Good-Night Giggles and Grace

God hears everything, but how is your royal hearing? Whisper, "God hears me. Can you?" to your mom. Can she hear you? Take turns whispering back and forth. Whisper a little quieter each time. How quietly can you whisper and still be heard?

Dear God,
I thank You, Lord,
For this day
And for listening
Each time I pray.
Amen.

Wonderfully Made by God

You made my whole being. You formed me in my
mother's body. I praise you because you made me
in an amazing and wonderful way. What you
have done is wonderful. I know this very well.
—Psalm 139:13–14

Who made your pajamas? Take a look at the label and see. Who made your favorite teddy bear? The tag will tell you. Now, who made you? Can you find your tag? Of course not! Princesses don't come with tags or labels. But the Bible does tell who made you— God did.

God created you with His very own hands, right in your mom's tummy. God made your eyes and your nose, your fingers and toes. He created your ears and your chin, and even your giggles and grins. God made you just the way He wants you.

And when He was finished, do you know what He said? God said, "You are wonderfully made!"

Good-Night Giggles and Grace

Are you sure you don't have a tag or a label? Does Mom? Or Dad? Play a tickly game to see if you can find any tags or labels. Could there be one under your chin or between your toes? Maybe it's hiding in your belly button—or right under your nose!

> Thank You, God, for toes that wiggle
> And tickly ribs that make me giggle.
> Thank You, God, for legs that run,
> And thank You most for the gift of Your Son.
> Amen.

Rest Your Heart

"Come to me, all of you who are tired and have heavy loads. I will give you rest."
—Matthew 11:28

When your body gets tired, you need to sleep. But what about when your heart gets tired? What if you are tired of being a good little princess? Maybe you're worried that you just can't share one more toy or obey one more rule. Maybe you just want to give in and give up.

Jesus understands that it's not always easy to be good—especially when you're tired. That's why He tells you to ask Him for help. Spend a little time talking to Jesus. Tell Him all your troubles and worries. Just as sleep rests your body, time with Jesus rests your heart and gives you peace—the perfect bedtime gift!

Good-Night Giggles and Grace

Do you have a special bedtime routine? If not, give this one a try:

With a great big stretch and a little yawn,
It's time to sing our good-night song.
Butterfly kisses and Eskimo nosies
Make you feel warm all down to your toesies.
So jump in bed and snuggle up tight.
Then say your prayers and say good night!

Dear God,
As I close my eyes to rest
And off to sleep I go,
I know that I am truly blessed—
And loved more than I know!
Amen.

Index